Los Duros

Manuel Luis Martinez

FLORICANTO PRESS

Floricanto Press
7177 Walnut Canyon Rd.
Moorpark, California 93021
(415) 793-2662
(800) 523-3175
www. FloricantoPress. com
ISBN:13: 978-1497473553
*"Por nuestra cultura hablarán nuestros libros. Our
books shall speak for our culture."*

Roberto Cabello-Argandoña, Editor

Reach the author at: www.manuelmartinez.info
Or: memorybabe2@yahoo.com
See: www.facebook.com/LosDurosNovel for teaching resources, study guides,
interviews, and photography.
Author photo credit: Molly S. Martinez

Cover photo credit: Manuel Luis Martinez

For Molly, love of my life, on whom I depend
to help me recognize Truth,
and for Cora, our daughter.

Acknowledgments

Thanks to David Wright, Lee Martin, and Jon Wei for their invaluable and instructive insight. I am eternally grateful for the financial support of Ohio State University, the MacDowell Colony, the Dobie Paisano Ranch, and the Ralph Johnston Fellowship. I couldn't have completed this book without their generosity. Thanks goes to my wife, Molly, who is always my first reader and who first suggested that I write about this very real place. Most importantly, I must express gratitude to the kids of Mecca and Thermal whose lives touched me. They allowed me to see things very few ever see. They fill me with optimism even during the darkest days of xenophobia and bigotry. Lastly, thanks Felipe Vargas and Rogelio "the Messiah" Garza: selfless teachers, and undaunted miracle workers in the desert. They deserve much more than my acknowledgment.

"How could you give me life, and take from me all the inappreciable things that raise it from the state of conscious death? Where are the graces of my soul? Where are the sentiments of my heart? What have you done, oh, Father, What have you done with the garden that should have bloomed once, in this great wilderness here?"

Charles Dickens, *Hard Times*

PROLOGUE

He always thought of her when he drove past the windmills. White towers of powerful blades turning serenely in the desert heat, hundreds, maybe thousands, so many that it looked as if the sun-baked mountains on which they sat would one day fly off into the spotless blue sky. As a young child, he'd imagined that on those searing white days, that it might be possible for the land to take flight, and if he were vigilant enough, for him and his mother to be on the spot when it happened. She'd been pleased by the idea when he mentioned it to her on a trip they took to Los Angeles for the funeral of a distant cousin. She'd told the child that his cousin was in heaven and that God had taken her there. He'd asked how God took people to heaven and she'd told him that the spirit flew on white wings right through the top of the blue sky. They'd been driving through the windmill highway and he'd believed it, and watching out the window, he told her that someday the land would fly to God as well. She'd liked that, he remembered.

And so when he drove past the windmills, he thought of his dead mother. One night, she didn't come home from work. He didn't notice until the morning when she usually woke him for school. He didn't like school and she encouraged him by waking him gently and putting his socks on for him. Then she'd make him breakfast.

But that morning, he'd awoken to find that she was gone. He'd been more puzzled than worried. He was used to the unusual. Nothing ever went the way it should in Los Duros. It had been that way since he was born. So he'd dressed himself and walked to the bus stop. He'd even fixed himself something to eat. There was no phone, no real address for them to notify him at home, so they came to the school. The principal called him out of class, and as soon as he saw the police, he knew it was bad. The police never brought anything good. They told the boy that a drunk driver had killed his mother on her way home from work. One of the casinos, a drunken gambler driving the wrong way on the street. After, the principal made some calls and then drove him home. The boy hid when child services came knocking. A few neighbors brought food and condolences. He wanted neither.

He took care of himself. He knew how to work, how to survive. He quit dreaming. That was the key. He told himself this every day. It was for the weak, for the soft. Memories were for suckers. So he closed off her room and commanded himself to stop thinking about her. Except for when he passed the windmills. He couldn't help it and there was no way to look past the thousands of lazily spinning fans. It was as close as he got to praying for her soul, as close as he ever allowed himself to dream.

He imagines that the rain that came after the accident washed the blood off the highway, into the sands. And he knows that somehow the whole of it, death, love, sadness, pain, and loss, is there, tethered to the mountains, the deadly road, the towering windmills which will never take flight toward the indifferent sun.

Los Duros

1.

There was nobody waiting for me outside the gate at Soledad. Just the heat coming off the fields of crops and heavy machinery. You'd think that a new release would do all he could to put some miles between himself and the jail he's been holed up in. But I knew that would be a mistake. So I walked a short piece and sat down where I could look down the 101. I wanted to head south. That's where it all lay for me. But I decided to go north, fight the instinct to drift down the currents of my hope. I might've picked that up from a book.

You wouldn't even notice Chualar if you drove through it. It's a bus stop, a place where some train tracks crisscross, a spot for farm machinery to sit and rust. It was also a place for me to find some work. But most important it was a place where I'd have to stare at the same mountains, the same sun I'd had to stare out at from my cell for the better part of ten years. I'm not running. That was what I had to settle inside my own head. It's like picking strawberries or grapes. You pick your spot, and you move through it slowly, getting it all before you move on to the next thing. That much I've learned.

Chualar isn't too far away in miles. It took only a day

of solid driving to get to Mecca, where I now live. But it took me almost ten years to get here. Nine of them locked away in the Soledad Pen, a *pinto*, a *tecato*, a born loser. And then another year biding my time in Chualar. I could give you a long, sad story about my life. But I don't have a call to do that. I was there because I deserved it, although I don't know that there's many who deserve being locked up in a hole. You should know that I didn't kill anyone. At least not directly. I sold heroin and used it too. I got caught and I ended up in Soledad. Simple as that. I'd had plenty of chances to turn it around. What you'd call brushes with the law, but it never made a difference so long as I was using. And I could give you the rest of the junkie confessional and tell you how I threw it all away and hurt the people I love and how I found Jesus. It's all true, but it gets old hearing that, so I'll skip it except to tell how being in a cage makes you face up to some things and it makes you do some accounting. When you don't have *chiva* to keep you from doing that accounting, you recollect what it is you've done and there's nowhere to go with it. Nothing but dead ends. So you either let it drive you crazy, turn you into an animal like they want, or you make some kind of a plan.

I've come to the Coachella Valley, with its poor farming towns of Mecca, Thermal, and Coachella, after a year in the shadow of my old prison. It was long enough to prove my patience, long enough to get some money together. I bought this old pickup truck so I could make a living. It's a good way of getting to learn a place. I go by construction sites and ask the foreman if they need anything hauled away or dumped or taken to another worksite. I do it all day long.

It gives me time to think and to plan out my next move. At night, I make my way back to Mecca with all the other *mojados* and I sleep in the parking lot of Lenchos Grocery. It's not so bad. I talk to the fellows, listen to them tell their stories. It's a lot like prison only the bars are invisible. We know just how far we can go.

Just a hundred yards from the asphalt lot we sleep on are the railroad tracks, and the trains run all night long. The sounds make you feel lonely. It's when despair rides in and a man begins to count all his failures. I see things in the dark, faces of people from my past. My wife, who tried for longer than I want to remember, to keep me from destruction. She would stand in the doorway, this small woman, barely a hundred pounds, her brown face and dark eyes focusing all her anger because she wouldn't beg and saying, "You'll have to go through me." In those days, I'd grab her by the shoulders and shove her away if I needed. It wasn't all about being a junkie. At least I thought it was about more, about being a man, or something like that. But I know now that it was about being a junkie.

The parking lot is full of guys with stories like that. Lots of them have run from their lives, left wives and kids behind, parents and brother and sisters. They may not have done it for drugs, but they've got other reasons and they have to face them every night too. It's hot, and the asphalt stays hot all night. It fries in the sun all day and when you get around to claiming a spot, you put down cardboard or a piece of plywood to insulate yourself from the terrible heat. You throw a blanket or sleeping bag on top of that, and you walk into the grocery store and buy a sixer. I sleep in the bed of my pickup. That makes me a high-class tenant.

Tonight, a couple of the fellows I've met sit around with me. One of them has a small barbecue pit, the size of a sink basin, and we roast up a chicken. We drink beer. Each of them takes turns telling about their families back home. Enrique says he left behind three daughters and a wife. He hasn't seen them in months and he's worried about his old lady because she doesn't have any brothers and her father is dead. "It's not good to leave a woman alone for too long," he says. The other guy, Mario, a tall, stringy man with a mustache and straight black hair, says he just got married and his wife wants a baby. "I want to bring her," he says, "but what do you do with a woman in a life like this?" He looks around the parking lot as we nod. After a while, Mario goes off to lie down and think about his woman. Enrique drifts off towards the telephone booths where he gets in line for his turn to call home. He tries to call every night.

I don't tell anyone about my past. Just that I'm from Chualar and that I'm taking a turn following the grapes. I don't tell them that I've found where my son, Juan, lives and where he goes to school. That I drive by the school when it lets out, park across the street next to a grove of palm trees and smoke cigarettes while I watch the kids stream out into the buses or into cars where parents wait.

My kid is short like his mother. He's brown like her too. Not like me, a *güero* from a grandfather who was said to have been a Spaniard. He's got her eyes too. Not that I've gotten close enough to him lately to see them. Again, from memory, since he was only six or seven when I got sent away. He lives alone in a trailer, in that terrible place. Los

Duros, the locals call it. He takes care of himself. I know how he does it too. I've been following him around long enough to know that it's going to land him in the same place I was before too long. Another Mexican screwed for life.

Maybe nothing I can do. There was nothing anyone could do for me. It's like that. Take this guy that I work for sometimes. He runs the showers for the *mojados*, for me too. He's an O.G. from the *barrios* of Fresno, and he tells about getting his legs crushed in a head on collision back in '72. He says, "I was drunk, on speed, and who the hell knows what else when I hit that car. I woke up a month later with my leg bones broken in about two dozen places, held together by metal rods. Only thing I could think about was getting high. It wasn't till my third wife left me that I straightened out. Talk about slow getting the message, but it's like that."

His name is Leo. When he hired me he wanted to know two things: are you a drunkard and do you have a license. I drive a van on Mondays and Tuesdays. I make 8 bucks an hour. I pick up *migros* in Mecca, Thermal, and Coachella and drive them to the showers. Best way to pick up information. *Migros* have to get the word quick or they starve or worse. They're natural victims. No one knows who they are, where they're going, who they live with. Nothing. Most of the time not even their names. That means any crackhead who wants to hit them over the head with a pipe and take the 7 or 8 bucks in their pockets, will usually get away with it. What are they going to do? Call the police? So they have to look out by spreading the news, the rumors, any *chisme* they hear on the down-low.

That's how I picked up on where my kid was. All I had was the one letter my wife sent me a couple of years ago. She wrote about working at a casino and about Los Duros, a slum in the desert run by Indians. Leo drove me around to show me the ropes, and it turned out that the van made a stop outside Duros. It made me sick knowing I was so close.

I've never been good with plans. For a while before I got sent away, the longest job I ever kept was driving shotgun with a buddy of mine on some long hauls between Indianapolis and Texarkana. It was spotty, that work, but I liked it because I was always moving. But with the trucking I knew where I'd end up and when I'd be back. That was as close as I got to figuring things out long term. Being in prison will suffocate you if you think about it too much. Especially if you're the restless type and prison is full of restless types, both cops and *pintos*. People that've spent their lives forcing square pegs into round holes.

Every junkie, every reformed criminal, every alcoholic will tell you that they've seen the light. Like San Pablo, the scales have fallen. But nothing changes till you're tired. That's the simple truth. Till you're beaten. And I'm not talking about getting tenderized like a tough piece of meat. I'm talking hammered. I'm talking about realizing that there's no such thing as winning the game. Because it isn't a game.

The day I found Los Duros, I knew not to jump out of Leo's van and start knocking on doors for my son. I had to find out what I was going to do, because you don't know until something happens. You've got intentions and then you have what you actually do. Two very different things.

One day, after I've finished dropping the last load of *piscadores* at the showers, Leo takes me to get some food. I tell him, "You do a lot of things. Things you don't want to remember because to remember is to bury yourself." He wants to know more, but he doesn't ask. The thing is, sometimes I want to bury myself and so I remember the look on her face the first time I slapped her. The shock. No anger, which made it worse. She was pregnant, somewhere in the middle, and I'd taken some money the night before, and she confronted me. I wanted to obliterate her accusing look because she was my mirror. It was the look I would have given myself if I'd had the courage to stare into my own eyes. And I backhanded her a good one. Enough to knock her back into the door. She kept looking at me, her hand up to her mouth where I'd landed the slap, and I knew looking into her eyes that I'd broken something that couldn't be fixed. I didn't even try. I left.

When you start destroying your own life, you make excuses for the losses. You make yourself think that you've weighed the cost and that you're willing to sacrifice it: a job, the trust of a friend, the love of a good woman, your own child. The heavier the price, the deeper you're in. And always there's the *chiva* to give you relief. And one day you're in a cell and you get called into an office with some cop who tells you your wife is dead, killed in a car accident. And you see her brown eyes piercing through the darkness of your cell, and you remember the sound of your hand slapping her face, and there's nowhere to go.

Nobody who doesn't belong in Los Duros goes in. Only way you'd even know it was there is to follow a cloudy dirt road off one of the farm routes. There's a small hand-painted sign that reads:

YOU ARE NOW ENTERING

THE SANCHEZ-PORTILLO INDIAN

RESERVATION

Follow that for a couple of miles, and you see a dirt lot with some cars parked in front of an unpainted garage that's got a sign in front that says *Mechanic*. There's another building, practically a shack, with about four or five beat-up washing machines and dryers. It also has a hand-painted sign that reads *Lavandería*. There's an old woman in there who sits at a cash register and will sell you a loaf of bread or a six-pack. That's all there is to serve the 10,000 souls that live in the slum. I park my truck with the other cars in front of the mechanic, and I walk in the camp. I do it four or five times a week. I walk by my son's trailer. Most of the time it's empty. Last week, when I knew he was at school, I got curious and I went in.

There's not much in there. It stinks of piss because the toilet's not hooked up to anything. There's not much light. Everything is closed up and no air gets in or out. I don't think that my wife kept the place like this. It's worse than the cell I was in for all those years. His mother's room is closed up too. There's an old twin mattress on the floor. It's still got sheets. It's unmade, maybe since that last morning she left to go to work. There's a few things in there that a woman should have. A hairbrush and a small mirror, some clothes laid on a rickety chair. There's a vase with a peacock feather in it, blue as the sky. It's the only thing in there that's got beauty.

My son's room is no better. Another twin mattress on the floor. The only thing the kid has is a few pairs of sneakers, some athletic jerseys. He's got a boom box and a collection of CDs. Rancheras and that rap shit, mostly. I know he's got a piece somewhere in here. I've been following him long enough to know that he isn't wet behind the ears. I look around a little but don't find anything except a bag of pills he's got stashed in a small closet. The place was so sad, I had the urge to torch it. But that's the way with me. First thing that pops in my head is to destroy the ugly.

Leo made me go to the bank. He said it was crazy for me to keep my cash in my pickup. "You're asking for someone to bash your brains in." I told him I never had a bank account. So he went with me. Right on Main Street in Thermal, a little bank with one of those ATM machines. Leo was responsible for getting them to put it up. "You know how much those goddamn robbers at the check cashing joints charge?" he says. He's the *patrón* around here, make no mistake. He gets things done. He'll face anyone down who wants to get in the way, including the mayor. He's told me stories. He was with Cesar Chavez back in the day, a bodyguard during the Coachella lettuce strikes. He says back then, they came after them with shotguns and baseball bats. The growers were willing to break heads, lots of them, if it meant showing wetbacks that they weren't going to have a say in anything.

"We outlasted the bastards," Leo says. "Most of the growers got bought out a long time ago by Dole and Welch's and all the other agribusiness conglomerates." He points at the enormous fields we pass, "We're still here. Of course, we're still taking it up the ass."

"That's the way it's always been, the way it will always be," I say.

"Things come and go," he says. "Everything's got its own time and place. You take this war and the current bunch of assholes in office, from top to bottom. People will get sick of it eventually. Some heads will roll. Our people will get sick of the way they're treated. They'll start shipping us back just like in the old days. Operation Wetback, that's what it was called. Look it up. And then the anger will come out. You can shit on someone for a long time, if they're desperate. But when you start punishing their children, making sure that you rain down as much suffering as possible on the defenseless, then people get up in arms."

Leo has seen it all, so I suppose he's right. My grandparents and parents, they never made any trouble. They worked hard, loved family, tried to keep food on the table, and stayed out of people's way. They didn't want any truck with whites. "*Los Americanos que se vayan a la chingada,*" my grandfather used to say, and that summed it up. Leave the whites to their own bullshit. But then it gets to a point and folks got no choice. I wonder what it will get us. To my thinking, it won't get us much at all. I've learned not to force anything. Violence begets violence, and violence is a tricky thing. It isn't always about sticking a gun in someone's face. Most of the time, it's about forcing the square peg in the round hole.

Juan doesn't miss school. He's always there on time, and he hangs around afterwards. Lots of the kids do. Nowhere better to go, I guess. It's a nice school. Big and new, with round buildings made of stucco, so that it blends with grace into the surrounding desert. Palm trees dot the parking lots and main entrance. But if you watch closely, you'll note the security guards with guns. You'll see the gates made of wrought iron, bars with sharp points at the top, like spears. It makes me wonder if they are afraid of intruders getting in, or the students getting out.

You might ask why I don't just get the boy, why I don't drive up and tell him, I'm your father, and we're leaving this place. But leave to where? To what? I'm as much an orphan as my son. And what would he do anyway? Why would he get in the truck with me? He must blame me for things, for his mother's death, for his lot in life, for the hardships that he's had to endure on his own. And what answers do I have for him? No, forcing the issue is not the answer. I watched my father use force to keep my mother at heel, to keep her home, keep her from speaking up, keep her in tattered clothes, and keep her at the stove, on her knees. She stayed until the old man died. But her life was hell, a silent prison that turned her into nothing but an inmate, and my father into a dog-mean warden.

I don't mistake patience with passivity. I used to. No, I'm here to save my son, but that means studying. I'm here to watch closely, to learn what I can about the boy and his life, so that I can say the right things, and do the right things. I remind myself when I get frustrated by looking at the only thing anyone gave me during my stretch at Soledad, a painted handkerchief a buddy made me. It's got my likeness on it and underneath he wrote something that helped me come to terms with all that lost time.

Driving the van yesterday, I carried a father and his two sons to the showers. They'd been at it a while from the looks of it. They were wiry, dark from the sun, the two boys with bandanas tied around their heads. I asked them how long they'd been following the grapes. The father pointed at his eldest, "Since this one was old enough to work. We come every year. Then we go back with our money and put it into our own business. We put up fences." His two sons were content to let their father speak for them. The younger of the boys was about Juan's age and looked something like him. I wanted to ask the father how he'd done things right, how he'd kept his sons with him. How he'd earned and kept their respect.

In prison, respect centers on who is strong and who is vulnerable. You beat respect into the others. You command it through fear. But strength comes in many shapes. My wife was strong. I thought I was strong. I wonder what Juan thinks about strength. It is both the prison and the key to its locks. It locks you up and destroys you as often as it frees and creates. My father drank himself into his grave. He never talked much, never seemed to rest or sleep much. His word was final and never questioned. But he went alone, unloved by his wife and children. He was a stranger to me, perhaps to himself. And yet, he was strong.

I think about these things as I drive the van filled with men of all shapes and sizes, dirty and sweaty, tired, always tired, and I wonder about what their children say and think about them. They're not all good fathers, not all of them are good men. Some have run away from their responsibilities, have vowed in their hearts never to return home. Others have come to save their children, their wives, their homes. And yet, they are all here in this place. All of them laboring under the sun, all of them suffering the heat, the burned skin, the broken hands and backs of *las piscas*.

One of the things I think about is where I stand in all of this. I've tried it my father's way, I've tried it my own way through drugs and crime. I strong-armed my dead wife, struck at the darkness of my life, the constant "No" that seems always to have been the answer to my hopes, however modest or poor they might have been. I know what it hasn't gotten me, but I want to know what is still attainable. Is there a "Yes" out there for me, for my Juan?

§ § §

Yesterday Leo said, "You know Juan, you're no dummy. An ex-con, yes, a *pendejo*, no." He said he'd like to see me in his office down at the Community Empowerment Center. So this morning, I went to the showers early, cleaned up, shaved, put on some clean clothes. I've got an old pair of khaki pants from before I got sent away. They kept them for me while I was in the joint. They're loose, but I have a belt. "You come to work for me full time," Leo says. "You go on driving the van twice a week, but I want to send you out to check on projects, maybe even work a little with the organizers. See if you can't break through to some of the *piscadores*. We need them to know that if they'll join us and speak up, it'll be harder for these *pinche gabachos* to cheat and keep them scared."

It's not a lot of pay. Not nearly what I made selling *chiva* before Soledad, but it's the best honest money I've ever made. It's enough to get a small place, just a room at the YMCA for now. But if I take it easy and save, maybe a house. Something for me and my son. The Y is in Mecca. It's a new building, the nicest in the dusty town. It's a dull orange stucco deal. It's air-conditioned and there's a pay phone and a washer and dryer. They charge $85 a week. It's usually packed but Leo pulled some strings. He helped bring the Y to Mecca. It's been a long time since I've had a place to hang clothes. I bought a hot plate even though there's no cooking. I stick to grilled cheese. No one can smell that. I also have a small radio I listen to *rancheras* on. There's a few youngsters here, but mostly it's a retirement home for burnouts like me or old *piscadores* who've got no one to take care of them. A small social security check will keep you here and buy you some groceries.

It's a lucky break, meeting Leo and him taking an interest. It's been a long time since anyone showed any confidence in me. Every day I get to work early, even before Leo does and I wait out in my truck. I smoke a cigarette or two, drink coffee, and feel the sun coming up and making the desert hot all over again. "That's what I like to see— enthusiasm," Leo says.

There's a receptionist at the Community Empowerment

Center. Her name is Raquel and she's a younger woman, only thirty maybe. She's very welcoming. A woman, who judging by the lines around her eyes, has seen some trouble. She says, "Juan, I'm going to have to get you a key to this place so you can open up. You're always here before anyone." She smiles when she says this. Despite not wanting any kind of complications, I notice that she doesn't wear a wedding ring. One day, I'm smoking a cigarette and Raquel comes out. She asks for one and I hand her a Camel. She asks, "So why are you in Mecca?" It's a simple question but a complicated answer.

I haven't told anyone why I'm here, but for some reason, I want to tell Raquel. Perhaps it's just because I need someone to know and I sense that she'll understand what I'm doing here without me having to explain it all.

"I have a son," I tell her. "He's in school here. His mother died and I'm here to see him."

"You haven't let him know you're here yet?"

"Not yet."

"What are you waiting for?"

"The right moment."

"When will that be?"

"I don't know. I only know that there'll be a right moment. But things have to be right. I want to have a house that we can live in. I want him to know that I'm here to make amends."

"Amends for what?"

"Too many things to list," I say and throw away the butt of my dead cigarette.

Leo and I drive out to a patch of desert not far from the

showers, a short walk from the parking lot I was sleeping in only a few days ago. It is Leo's new project. He's overseeing the building of a park. "There'll be trees, grass, swings, even a running track with lights. There'll be basketball courts," Leo says pointing at the southern corner of the lot. "Kids got to have something to do, or they come up with *chingaderas* that only get them into trouble." He's proud of this new project. "You know how hard it is to get those *gabachos* on the city council to agree to give us land? To let loose a few dollars? All they care about is building new golf courses around here. New country clubs, new mansions for the rich in Indian Wells and Rancho Mirage. But if you keep getting up their nose, they'll throw you something." He lights a cigarette as we look out at the burning sand.

"My wife died a year ago. God fucked me good," he says. "She was sitting outside during a church festival. I left to feed my horses. She was going to get our daughter to drive her back. Instead I got a phone call from my girl telling me she'd had a heart attack. You want to hear the bitch of it all? My girl said that my Rosie told her, 'I'm tired,' and she closed her eyes and the last thing, 'I see Jesus.' My girl thought she'd gone to sleep. There I was, tending to my *pinches caballos*. Thing is, I don't know what to do with myself anymore."

I flick another cigarette butt in the sand. "This is good, all this." I point at the lot, at the park that will one day be there.

"Yes," he says. "If it weren't for the work, I'd eat the barrel of a shotgun."

"You've helped me," I say. But Leo gets embarrassed

and he says, "Let's get out of here. Too goddamned hot."

§ § §

My son is planning something. He and two of his crew have been casing a construction site. There's a ton of tile that's been delivered for a party house at a fancy apartment complex that's going up and they want to steal it. One of the boys works there. Why they think they can get away with it, I don't know. The last two nights, I've parked my truck close to the site, my lights off, only the orange cherry of my cigarette to give me away. I park under a palm tree and wait. Tonight, my head full of thoughts, I consider the palm tree. Its lonely beauty, its outside so hard, sharp, edged with blades. But palms are fragile. They don't just grow anywhere. Their roots are shallow, and they're easily destroyed. Their skin shields soft, pulpy interiors. They are like armed warriors with poetic souls. My Juan is like this, I think.

There is no moon, and a truck drives up to the site with its lights off. It slows on the opposite side of the lot, three hunched figures pausing to look around. They want to make sure that there's no security or police on the premises. One boy gets out. He's not Juan. He's dressed in a black T-shirt, a black Raiders cap covering his head. He walks to the tile quickly. He's nervous, but he gets to the pallets and looking around, signals for the driver to bring the truck over. Juan and the other boy get out, and the three survey the merchandise. These are heavy goods. They are amateurs. They don't even have work gloves. After a short discussion, they get after it and begin to load the tile onto the back of the truck. It takes two of them to lift one pack at a time.

I walk towards them as quietly as possible. When I'm about ten yards away, I turn on a flashlight and yell, "What are you doing there!"

They're surprised. The two carrying a package of tiles drop them, the ceramic crumbling dully when it hits the ground. They don't know whether to run or make a stand. They look quickly at Juan. He has sized me up. He sees that I'm no policeman.

"Hey, *ese*," he says. "You better get your ass out of here, or we're going to have to fuck you up."

The two boys are watching, nervous. This is more than they've bargained for.

"*Chale*," I say, "I don't think that's going to happen, but I've taken ass kickings in my day from bigger, better *vatos* than you."

Juan looks at me, his hand above his brow as he tries to figure out if he knows me.

"Who are you? I know you, man?"

"You should know me," I say.

"Let's get the fuck out of here," one of the boys says to Juan.

"Shut up," he says still looking at me. "Who the hell are you, *vato*?"

"I know you," I say. "Your name is Juan."

"How do you know that?" he asks, his hand coming down, his head drawing forward to get a better look.

One of the boys has gotten in the truck and started it. "C'mon, Juan," he yells, revving the engine. The other boy gets in quickly. "C'mon, dude," they shout. The truck rolls forward and Juan steps backwards to get in, but he holds his gaze on me.

"You better look out, fucker," he says defiantly. "Next time, I won't be with pussies."

I don't say anything. I just want them to leave. I want to be spared telling him who I am. I need more time. Following Juan around is going to be much more difficult now. Mecca and Thermal are small. Los Duros is smaller.

§ § §

Today Leo asks me if I'll drive his son to the VA hospital in Chula Vista. His son, Henry, lost both his legs in Iraq a couple of years ago. He's a nice enough kid, only a few years older than my Juan. But he can't look you in the eye, and his hands shake. He'll start talking about something and then he trails off, like he's forgotten what he was going to say. He's shaved his head, but it's been a week or two and his scalp is covered with dark bristle. On the way, he asks me how I like working for Leo. I tell him his old man is solid.

The whole drive, I don't want to bring up anything about the war, although I want to know how he deals with his wounds. Finally, he brings it up.

He says, "I hate the VA."

"Why?"

"Nothing but a bunch of chopped up *vatos*, that's why."

I don't know what to say to this. Henry is trapped in his own body. It's his prison. The rest of the way, he's quiet, pulling his baseball cap down below his eyes and pretending to fall asleep. We get to the VA a couple of hours later. I help him inside the hospital, but Henry doesn't want much help. He uses his arms to lift himself quickly, jumping into the chair when I bring it around the side. "I'm alright," he says as he wheels himself to the automatic doors. There's a dozen young men in the waiting room, all of them like Henry, missing legs and arms. One of the boys is missing half his face and you can see the burn scars on his neck and arms. It's terrible. Henry goes into see the doctor on his own and I walk outside to smoke. It's too sad to sit in the waiting room. For some reason, it makes me worry all the more for Juan. He's in a war zone too. Don't let anyone tell you that's not true. The government keeps sending young people, mostly blacks and Mexicans and poor whites, to get blown up. They scoop them out of these neighborhoods with promises that they can escape the shooting and death of the *barrios* by going to Iraq and facing the shooting and bombs over there. They trick them into trading one gang, one set of colors, for another.

After a long while, Henry comes out of the hospital. He looks tired. He lets me help him into the van. "Everything alright?" I ask.

"Alright as it's ever going to be," he says.

"How often do you come out here?"

"Every couple of months. At first, I was in here for almost a year. I had six operations on my legs before they got it right enough so I could get prosthetics. But I didn't take to them well. Infection and other problems. They want me to try again. I might. But in the end, you don't have legs.

It don't matter much whether its wheels or goddamn metal stilts."

Leo got his son a job working with younger kids in Thermal, so I change the subject to that.

"All I care about these days is making sure that they don't get one more Mexican from here. I don't want to see one of my kids come back like me, and for what? So these motherfuckers can get richer."

"I don't know much about politics," I say. "But I've seen enough to know that the ones at the top shit down the necks of the ones on the bottom. Prison will teach you that quick."

Henry says, "I wish I would've gotten pinched for the shit I did as a kid and sent to prison. I might be behind bars, but I'd be walking."

I don't argue with Henry. But I wanted to add that the world or God, whoever or whatever, has all kinds of ways of chopping up people. I met lots of cripples in the joint, men even more damaged then Henry, cut up, burned, beat up by life so that they're useless to themselves or anyone else. There ain't no prosthetic for your soul.

An hour outside of Mecca, I notice a cop following. He wants to stop me, I can tell. Cops always have a sixth sense about ex-cons. They smell it. They can see it in the way you drive your car, in your walk, in your eyes, maybe how you shrink back when you see a uniform. Don't let any of those prison movies fool you. It's the uniforms that control the joint. They control the yards, they control the cells, where and when you eat, work, exercise, spit, shit, or sit. Sure enough, he turns his lights on just after I notice him. I tell

Henry, "Relax, we're getting pulled over." Henry keeps his hat slung over his eyes.

The cop steps out slow, his ticket book on a small metal clipboard, a *gabacho*, taking his time, reading the plates, checking out the parking lights. He wants to make us nervous. I keep my hands on the wheel as he sidles over to the driver's window. "Driver's license and registration," he says. He's a prick, a tall, ex-footballer whose gut has gone to fat, plenty ready to give me a hard time. I pull out my wallet slowly, telling him, "My registration is in the glove box." He looks over the stuff long and hard and handing them back says, "How long were you in the joint for?"

"Long enough," I say.

"Long enough to know better, right?" He flashes a light in my eyes. "You been drinking tonight?"

"No," I say.

"What you doing on the road so late? Sure you haven't been having a few at the casinos? Might as well tell me the truth."

I swallow hard, trying to calm myself. "I'm driving my friend back from the hospital."

"What's wrong with your friend?" he says looking at Henry who's still slumped in his seat, his eyes beneath his cap. "Hey, mister, you awake?"

Henry stirs, lifting his cap. "What is it," he says.

"You alright?" the cop asks. "Looks like you're nodding off there."

"Just resting. There a law against that?"

"Depends," the cop says. "Give me the keys to the van, nice and slow," he tells me. "I'm going to run plates and warrants." I give him the keys. "Keep your hands where I can see them," he says turning back towards his squad car.

"Fucking pigs," Henry says.

"Just keep calm," I tell him. "He's just showing us who's boss. We'll give him the yes sir, no sir routine and he'll leave us be."

"Fuck him," Henry says.

After a few minutes, the cop comes back. "This van's not registered to you. How come you're driving it?"

"It's my boss's van. I told you, I was driving my friend to the hospital. The owner is his father."

"That right?" the cop asks. Henry doesn't look at him. "I said, 'that right?'" the cop asks him directly.

"Man, why don't you fucking hassle someone else? There's plenty of drug runners and coyotes running *mojados* on this highway. You should look for them instead of giving us trouble."

The cop smiles then. "That's right. That's exactly why I'm checking you out. I got me an ex-con driving a van that isn't registered to him and a loudmouth hiding behind a baseball cap."

"Sir," I say trying to keep the cop from going off, "this man's a war veteran. We're coming back from the VA."

"What's that to me?" he says. "I didn't sign him up, did I?" He's staring directly at Henry now, hoping that he'll say more. When he doesn't, the cop hands my license back. "I ought to drag both your asses out of the van and give you sobriety tests. I could get a K-9 unit out here in five minutes, go over the vehicle. Your pal is giving me probable cause."

I sit there, with my hands on the wheel my guts in knots,

sweating and fidgeting, back in jail. He writes me a ticket for not using my signal on a lane change. I guess I did it. I don't know for sure. He tears it off the pad. He looks back at Henry. "I don't have time to be messing with cripples tonight. Make sure you keep your nose clean, jailbird." He walks back to his car and takes off.

I get back on the road. I can't look over at Henry. "Goddamn fucker," he says under his breath, and I look over enough to see his eyes staring at the rearview mirror, his left hand clenched. "Goddamn it," he says sounding angry enough to cry.

Finally, I say, "Sorry about that. I shoulda been driving more careful." He sits there for a second, then, "You don't have anything to be sorry about. You want to know what there is to be sorry about? I was in country for two days when on patrol, my partner, he spots a kid, shoots him in the back, just like it was no more than shooting a dog. Just blows the kid away. I freaked, told him, 'oh shit, man, this is bad. We got to get a story straight. You fired a warning shot first, okay?' And he looks at me like I'm from fucking Mars. And he says, 'no one gives a goddamn out here, Hank.' And he was right. So you hold on to your apologies for someone else, brother."

We don't talk after that. I drive him back to Leo's house, get back in my truck and drive back to the Y slow and careful, like I'm driving a truck full of eggs. I get to my room, shut the door and pour myself a glass of Wild Turkey Leo gave me this morning as a thanks for driving his kid to the hospital. I have the shakes and I can't think of anything to do except sit in the dark and drink, thinking about how they'll never take their foot off our necks.

§ § §

Juan spotted me today. I knew it would be harder to keep my head down after I confronted him and his crew the other night. But it was dark, and my truck had been parked far enough away that I didn't think they'd notice it. But still, I shouldn't have used his name like I did. It's sure to tip him off if he thinks hard enough. Even though I don't like it, maybe that's the way it's got to happen. Like I said before, I'm not forcing anything. If he's supposed to find out his father is back like this, then that's the way it's going to happen. So I've got no choice. Any day that I don't see him, I feel like it's a wasted day. That it signals that I'm here for my own good and not his. I'm not supposed to be rebuilding my life for me. It's supposed to be for him.

He looked at me, where I was parked in the usual spot next to the grove of palm trees across from the school. He eyeballed me for a couple of minutes and then waved one of his boys over and talked to him while they both looked in my direction. Free country, right? So I didn't sweat it, didn't move. Sooner or later, I figured, it would all come out and so how or why should I run from it? But they didn't make a move. They stood there for a while, until someone drove up in an old Monte Carlo. They got in and took off squealing tires, regular little gangsters.

I think Raquel is interested. At work, she makes sure to go outside when I'm out there smoking. When I get back from driving the showers, she takes note. She makes mostly small talk, but she drops in things about her ex-husband and how he's in Texas now, and how she doesn't have kids. Things like that. She has some education, went to junior college for three years and got an associates in bookkeeping. She says she wants to go back.

"You want to leave this place?" I ask her over a cigarette.

"Not really. I grew up here. I tried moving away before. Met my ex in L.A. Never got anything from that city except him, and all he brought me was misery, debt, and a load of busted lips."

"I'm sorry about that," I say. "That's not right."

"Lots of things aren't right. Doesn't mean they can be avoided."

"I'd tend to agree with you, but I hope that you're wrong," I tell her.

She looks at me for a couple of seconds. "You're cryptic," she says.

"What's that mean?"

"It means you keep a lot to yourself and what you do doesn't quite add up all the time."

"I'm sorry about that too," I tell her. "I guess I learned that not many people want real answers to anything."

"Are you saying you don't think I really care?"

"No," I said. "Not that. Just that I've been away for a long time. Almost ten years and in prison, no one gives a shit about your hard luck story. They've got their own."

"What happened?" she says. "I mean, if it's not too personal."

"Too many things," I say.

"See, that's what I mean about being cryptic."

"Oh," I say lighting another cigarette. "Maybe I'll tell you some time. Nothing you need to worry about." I smile then. "Anyway, we should probably get back to work."

"You just lit another cig," she says.

"Yeah," I say and throw it on the ground, grinding it out with my boot. "When we have more time."

"How about we go get something to eat after work? We'll have plenty of time that way." She smiles halfway, a little afraid that I'll shoot her down. And the thought comes into my head. It's my instinct to pull back like a startled turtle. But I don't.

"Yeah, let's do it."

She smiles and says, "I know a great place out in Rancho Mirage. It's not that far."

I spend the rest of the day driving the showers, but the whole time thinking about why I said yes to Raquel. It isn't smart to get involved with a woman. I don't know where I'm going or what I'm going to do yet. My whole focus is on Juan and that's the way it's supposed to be. I get confused sometimes because as much as I want things to happen—the good things, my son, a home, a life, maybe making amends in this life—other things get in the way. That's the way it's always been for me. Maybe for most people. I start out with the right intentions and I get sidetracked. That's why I find myself in the mess that I'm in now. That's why my son is running the streets in danger of getting killed or screwing his life up. But I get confused because here's this woman, and she is a good person. She has a good heart. I can see that. And maybe she's here so she can help me learn something. Maybe I'm here so that she can learn something from me. Who am I to question the paths that are presented to me? That means I have to live right. I have to keep my eye on the prize.

So at the next stop, I head for the phone booth and I call the office and Raquel answers. It's good to hear her voice and I feel a pang of sadness and desire in my stomach. But I take a drag of my cigarette and I tell her that something's come up.

"I can't make it after all," I tell her.

"Everything okay?"

"Yeah, don't worry."

"Okay Mr. Cryptic," she says trying to hide her disappointment. "But how about some other night?"

"Yeah," I say, "some other time." I hang up and push away the sadness. I have to keep my mind clear.

§ § §

Leo works overtime getting money to keep the showers going. He calls the Mayor's office, calls the local businesses that all depend on migrant labor, the construction companies, the big grocery chains, the growers unions, the non-profits and agencies. "I'll even talk to the casino *indios*," he says. He's got to find $15,000 every three months to keep the electricity and water running. It isn't easy. No one wants to part with money.

"The poor always have to go begging," Leo says. "It doesn't matter if it's kids or widows. The world doesn't give much of a tinker's damn. We got kids living in these parts with lung disease and cancers from the pesticides and the toxic dumps and all the illegal burning. As long as they keep away from the country clubs and the golf courses, these rich fucks don't care. And the middleclass *gabacho*s, they've been scared shitless by the media and the politicians with their lies about illegals coming to take their social security away."

Next to the Y, there's a community clinic where a nurse shows up a couple of times a week. There's usually a line, young mothers with skinny babies, old people with diabetes and pneumonia, all of them too poor to get even the minimum. Leo says that the government's got them scared. "It's gotten to the point where some of these people will practically let their kids die rather than take them to the emergency room for fear that they'll be put in prison or sent back to Mexico." He takes a look at me. "When's the last time you saw a doctor?" he asks.

"Prison," I say.

"You ought to get that cough looked at."

He means that I'm always smoking and hacking when I do. "Yeah, one of these days," I say.

Leo also oversees the clinic. The Center raises money for the equipment and the testing.

"Well, get over there and get yourself checked out," he says. "I'd like to know how things go there when I'm not around anyway."

The next day, I show up bright and early at the small clinic. There's already people waiting. One of the kids, a boy, maybe four or five, reminds me of my Juan when he was that age. He's sick. His eyes are yellow, and he doesn't move much or cry. He sits next to his mother, a skinny young girl. The boy's legs are chunky little drumsticks and he has Popeye forearms. He is dark brown with curly hair and he's dirty, with runny eyes and nose. He wears a dingy T-shirt too small for him, and stained mismatched shorts. He doesn't have shoes. His mother's a teenager. They live in Mecca. The boy's no different from the thousands like him that live here, but to someone, he is special.

After an hour, the nurse calls for me. She takes a listen to my chest, has me breathe deep and cough. She asks me how much I smoke. There's no reason to lie.

"You smoke two packs a day," she says shaking her head. "That's terrible for you."

"It'd be much more terrible if I didn't," I tell her.

"Well, you should know that you're in the beginning stages of emphysema," she says like she's concerned.

Everyone picks how they die. Some do it quick, some others take their time, eating bad shit, smoking, drinking, screwing strangers. We're all suicides in that way. But adults make their own choices, in so far as they can. Children don't. They get pulled here and there, from one country to the other, from one shack to another, from field to field. They get sick and have no choice in their parents' bad luck. They are orphaned in this land, by parents, by families, by the community, by the church, by the politicians. Not even God cares. I light up another cigarette out in the parking lot.

"What did the nurse tell you," Leo asks later in the day.

"She says I'm fine."

He says, "If you're fine, then I'm sure to live forever."

Yesterday I saw a deportation. A bus, with Border Patrol written across its side in big black letters, led by two ICE squad cars, drove onto a field. They got out and began to call on the *piscadores* to come out of the rows. "Do not run," a big officer said into a bullhorn. They lined them up, about 40 men and women, some old, some young. It was the hottest part of the day, and the workers were sweating and tired. Most of them were made to get on the bus as the agents checked them out. A foreman came over and he was given a citation or something. Who knows? No one argued, except for a young worker who kept claiming he was a citizen. He was let go after a while. The rest went meekly to who knows where. I don't know who this served exactly. Three dozen workers, stinking in the hot sun, tired and dehydrated, picked up and taken without the chance to tell their families anything, all because they were picking vegetables. They'll be questioned, have their pictures taken, perhaps finger printed. Then they'll get shipped off. Somewhere someone will write a story about it in a newspaper. Somewhere some *gabacho* will read it and feel some kind of vindication because these poor fuckers are even more miserable. The foreman will curse his luck, send the citation to the corporation that owns the field, and then hire himself a brand new crew tomorrow. It's all a joke, that is, to everyone but the workers and their barefoot, snot-nosed *chamacos*.

§ § §

Leo is giving me a raise. He wants me to keep track of

the park construction site, to maintain the showers, to hire a new van driver and supervise him. He wants me to be at the office whenever I'm not keeping track of the projects.

"You learn fast," he says. "I like that. You keep at it, so I'm making you my chief assistant. I need to slow down and I like having someone around who can answer questions and handle situations when I'm not here."

There's enough money now that I can think about moving from the Y into a small rental house I've had my eye on. It's in Coachella. It's not in the nicest neighborhood, but the houses on the street are neat and kept well. The house is white with green trim. There is a small yard in front and there are some palm trees and even a rose bush. The rose bush makes me think of Raquel. There are two bedrooms and I imagine Juan coming to live there and taking his place in one of them. There is a small kitchen where I could cook and even a washing machine. The best thing, though, is that there's a small patio in the back that is covered. The man will rent it to me for $500 a month. I ask Leo to advance me enough to pay a deposit. When I sign the papers, for the first time, I feel like maybe things will go right.

After the man leaves, I go to the Wal-Mart and buy two cheap plastic lawn chairs, green like the trim of the house. I put them on the porch and sit and imagine that me and my boy will one day sit there together. I fear it's too much to hope for.

Raquel wants to see the house. She's even more excited than me. "We'll go see it during lunchtime," she tells me, leaving no room for objection. Not that I would, because I have to admit that I'm anxious for her to see it. I feel proud that I've done something right. We drive there in my truck. The house is only a couple of miles from the Center. Raquel is sweet about it all. She says, "Wow!" when she sees the place. "This is nice. It's so well-maintained."

"There's a porch," I can't help saying. "It's around the back."

We walk through the house and Raquel tells me that it is bright and cheerful. "And this kitchen, very nice to cook in. When are you moving in?" she asks.

"I have moved in," I tell her.

"Where are your things?"

"That's it," I say pointing at the two lawn chairs that I've brought into the living room. I've put a TV tray between them. My radio sits on the tray.

She walks into the bedroom. "Is that your bed?" she says looking at the small blow up mattress.

"Yes."

"It doesn't look very comfortable."

"Better than I had in the joint."

"You know, there's a lot of used furniture stores around here," she says putting her hand on my arm. "There's a Goodwill too. You'd be amazed at what the rich people donate around here. You could probably find a couch and a real bed, even a chest of drawers."

"I don't need all that," I say.

"You could make it very comfortable here. Especially if you want your son to come live with you."

I look around the place. Finally I say, "It could use some

cheering up, I guess." Raquel looks at me, her hand still on my arm. She smiles and then she kisses me on the cheek. She is happy.

We make plans to go look around after work. I drive her back and stay outside for a smoke. She walks into work smiling about how she's going to help me. And I can't help but to watch her because kindness is rare in this world, and because she makes me feel like things are going to work out.

After work, we drive to Rancho Mirage. It's another world, this place. With its wide streets and walls that keep the undesirables out. People like me and Juan, Leo and Henry. Every other block is a golf course or country club with security guards parked at the entrances. The stores have manicured lawns, lots of them with fountains that splash clear water, a paradise if you've got the money and the right skin color. Mostly there's expensive cars driven by middle-aged white men with expensive watches and golf shirts. The shitty broke-down clunkers from Mecca and Thermal don't exist here. All the places have Spanish names, like the people behind the registers of the gas stations and grocery stores.

Raquel says, "It's pretty out here, isn't it?"

"It's okay."

"What's the matter?"

"Nothing," I say fumbling with the lighter. It's nearly out of fluid. Finally I get it to strike a flame. "It's just that all these walls remind me of prison. I haven't seen these many guards in front of stone walls since I got out of the joint."

Raquel says, "You have to break out of that mind set."

Then she looks embarrassed, like she said something she shouldn't have.

"What do you mean?"

"Never mind. We're getting close to the Goodwill," she says looking to her left.

"No, tell me. I can take it. If you've got something to say, just say it."

"Don't get angry," she says as we pull into a small parking lot.

"I'm not mad. I just want you to finish your thought. It might help me."

"It's just that if you see a wall everywhere, I mean, if that's all you see, walls, then you'll always be in prison. There's a lot more to see around here than those obnoxious resorts. Let me tell you, I understand what it feels like to walk around here with brown skin. I grew up here. From Palm Springs to Indio, it's the same thing. We're either invisible or a danger, but if you give into that mentality, then you adopt it and you start seeing the world the way they want. I just think you need to understand that, maybe try and break away from the things you've been taught to see and understand."

"I know what I know," I tell her.

"Okay, it's just some advice. We should've just dropped it."

I look out my window. There's a smudge. The day seems hotter and the trip to find cheap furniture seems pathetic now. "Look," I say, "I'm not mad and I'm glad we didn't drop it. I like people to be honest. I don't blame anyone for my life or my mistakes, for the bad things I've done.

Maybe these people got a right to feel scared. Maybe not. Maybe it's us who ought to be afraid of them. Either way, things sort themselves out. Only thing is, I know you can't wall anything out. You can't wall out trouble or sickness or death. You can't wall out crime or drugs or hate. Shit happens, and as far as evil is concerned, I found out a long time ago, that every human heart is sick with it. So for these people to think they can wall out the ugly, well it's just a pipe dream. A pipe dream every bit as useless as a junkie trying to keep the pain out by stabbing his veins."

"I'm sorry," she says. She puts her hand on my shoulder. It feels strange, like something I should get away from at the same time that I want to take her hand in mine and tell her that she doesn't have to apologize to me.

Instead, I just say, "It's alright. We're just talking."

The store is pretty big, filled with clothes and shoes and all kinds of stuff. I take a look at myself in a mirror, noticing how shabby I look. Still wearing the same khakis I've had since I got here, a plaid shirt, one of three, and boots that are showing their age, the leather cracked, the heels worn down to nubs. Raquel spots me looking at the clothes.

"You should get a few things while you're here."

"Oh yeah? Am I out of style?" She laughs, but not mean, just friendly agreement.

She helps me pick out a couple of pairs of jeans and a couple shirts. Last, a new pair of boots. "You should get some dress shoes too," she says.

"I don't go to church."

"Not for church," she says. "You never know when you'll want to take a girl out."

I let it drop, pretending like I'm looking at the prices of the boots. When we're done with that, we go back to the furniture. They don't have a lot, but they've got mattresses that aren't too bad, a few tables, even a chest of drawers that's in good shape. I debate buying two mattresses, but settle on one. The *vato* in the store helps me load the stuff on the truck. We tie it down. On the way back, she says, "What's going to be the best thing about living in your own house?"

"That's easy," I say. "Not washing my socks in the sink. I didn't even have to do that in prison." She laughs. "Seriously though, I think it's this new feeling I've got, when I pull into the driveway, and it sinks in that I've got the key and it's my place. I can sleep in the bathroom, or eat in the bedroom. Hell, just being able to move from one room to another, that's something I haven't had in more than ten years," I say. Raquel nods. Telling her these things makes them real for me, something else that I like about her.

"You know, in the joint," I tell her, "I used to sit in my cell and stare at the bars, sometimes for hours. I don't like tight spaces. And I'd just look at them, not because I wanted to, but because they were like magnets for my eyes. They were there, real and hard and they weren't going nowhere. There was this guy named Curtis, a dude who'd killed someone in an armed robbery, a crackhead, at least on the outside, a guy who'd cut your head off if he wanted something from you. He went crazy in there. Tried to go through the bars one night. Just kept banging his head into the bars like he could push his flesh and bone through the steel. Doesn't make sense, right? But there were a lot of times I thought about doing the same thing."

"I can't imagine frustration like that."

"He was nuts," I say. "But still, frustration, that's it. Frustration. Still though, at least you could see the bars in prison. Just like I can see these walls. I know what they meant, knew what my limits were. For a prisoner, there's no mistaking that. Out here, though, it's a lot trickier. A lot more frustrating."

"I guess so," she says. "Maybe I do understand it a little. Don't go breaking your head though."

"Nah," I laugh. "I'm not there, not yet."

She wants to help me move the stuff, but I don't let her. "You'll mess your nice work clothes up."

"These things? No. And look," she says pointing down at her feet, "I've got comfy shoes on. You're not talking to the Queen of England here. I'm not worried about breaking a nail."

"Nah, you just go on home. I'll manage. Nothing in here's too heavy. I've got experience moving furniture out of houses." She doesn't get the joke. When I drop her off at her car, I can tell she's disappointed. I hurt her feelings, pushing her away. It makes me feel bad, but I know it's for the best. For me, for Juan, for her.

I go home. Home. I set up the new furniture, taking my time to put it where I think it looks best. I move things around, the dresser on this side of the room and then on that side of the room. I put the mattress under the window that looks out at a palm tree. Late at night you can see the moon while you lay there thinking. When I'm done, I sit in the lawn chair and feel satisfied that even though it ain't much, I got it through my own labor, that piece by piece, it's coming together.

§ § §

He spots me again. This time he comes across the street, two of his friends in tow. He walks like he has something to prove, shoulders squared, arms slightly out and held motionless. Juan comes up to my truck. I sit still, a cigarette in my left hand and as he walks up, I look at him through the open window.

"Why the fuck you stalking me, old man? I know you or are you a fag?" His friends smirk and one of them elbows another.

I don't say anything for a minute. I take a drag of the cigarette to think it through. I've thought about this moment a lot, all the time I was in prison, all the time I've been here. Always the scene was different, playing itself out like some sappy episode of a *telenovela*.

"What the fuck, man, you don't hear so well? You been following me. We got some business I don't know about?"

"Maybe," I say. "I'm your pops." For a second, he looks confused, the machismo slipping a little, letting me see the boy under the front. I see him for the first time like I remembered him in prison, my boy Juan. His eyes harden their focus after a few seconds. He looks me over. His friends aren't smirking anymore. They're looking me over now.

"I ain't got no father," Juan says. He realizes that this might sound soft, and now he scowls at me. "And it sure wouldn't be a sorry-ass motherfucker like you. Why don't you get the fuck outta here?"

I look at him and don't say anything. I'd planned all the things I'd say. I thought that he would give me a chance to explain or ask me some questions and that I'd be able to come up with answers that made sense. But there isn't anything right now.

"Go on, *vato*," he says backing up. "Don't let me catch you coming around here no more. Next time I won't warn you." One of his crew, a tall skinny *pendejo*, says, "Yeah, we'll bomb on your ass." Juan looks at him hard, and he shuts up.

"You don't have to believe it, but I'm your pops," I say again. "And I'm not going anywhere, Juan."

"Fuck you, man," Juan says. "You're crazy." And they go back across the street. On the other side, Juan turns back and looks at me again, quickly, confused. He is angry and I don't hold it against him. I start the truck and pull out, the dust swirling as the tires spin till they catch hold.

That night, I go over it again and again. It didn't go the way I wanted it to. But then again, I'm not sure how else it could have gone. Things happen the way they happen. You can't control that. Patience isn't a virtue, it's a lesson. It's a series of lessons. You learn that in prison and those who don't learn it wind up killing themselves in one way or another, just like banging your head against the bars.

Raquel calls me. She wants me to meet her for dinner. We end up in Coachella, not far from my house. She wants to know how things went.

"Not so good," I say.

"All you said was I'm your father?"

"That's all I could think of."

"Hmm, sounds a little Darth Vadery. What about, let's go get something to eat, or let's talk. Or I love you?"

"That wouldn't work," I say.

"How do you know?"

"I just know. I've been around hard cases all my life. You don't say that kind of thing to a boy."

"That's stupid," she says. She gets angry. "Do you know how stupid that is?"

"He's my son," I say. "I don't want to talk about it anymore."

"Well, you're my friend, and I care about you and you've got to stop with all this macho bullshit. You should've jumped out of that truck and wrapped your arms around him."

"You don't think I wanted to," I say. She doesn't say anything to that. "You don't think I've been waiting for ten years for that? Why do you think I'm here? You think I'm skulking around town, driving these *mojados* to the showers because I like it?"

She drops her gaze, embarrassed because I got a little loud. "Look," she says, "I'm sorry. It's just that I get frustrated hearing things like that. My father, he wasn't the best or worst of men. He worked all day long at a mechanic's shop, came home, drank a few beers and never said anything to anyone, not even my mom. Never told us kids anything about himself. My brother dropped out of school. My father stayed silent. He joined a gang. My father kept quiet. My brother got into all kinds of trouble and the old man never said a word. Finally, my brother joined the army and shipped out. Never a word from my father, nothing. And you don't think that ate us all up? And the worst part is, I don't know why he kept quiet, don't know what he was thinking or feeling. So we spent our lives guessing, always guessing, never knowing what he wanted or what he expected or if he gave a good goddamn. So when you tell me that you couldn't think of anything to say, or you didn't want to show him up in front of his friends, or whatever it is that you were thinking, it still comes up to the same thing. You didn't say anything. You didn't let him know."

"I'm not going to force anything," I tell her quietly. She doesn't understand and I can't explain it to her. She drops it and we eat our food in silence.

§ § §

He's following me. It's his turn to hide in the shadows, to watch and bide his time. Does he believe me? Maybe. Or maybe he wants to find out what my game is. But he's got to know. A son knows his father. He's changed, but I haven't changed all that much since he was five or six. The last time I remember seeing him was after they sent me to Soledad. His mother brought him once. I remember that he was scared, just a little kid wearing a red T-shirt and funny shoes with a Scooby on them. I remember he wouldn't come to me. He stayed close to his mother. I tried to talk to him, but he wasn't having it. My wife kept telling me, "*tiene miedo.*" I don't know if it was me he was afraid of, or the joint. Probably both.

Never say never is rule number one for junkies. You go into it thinking it's just about the high and then you find out that it's about everything. Getting the high, The Calm, becomes everything. And one day, after chasing it for so long, you find that now it's chasing you. All day long, you're either scoring, trying to score, or feeding the buzz. And as your life becomes more and more chaotic, and you start to destroy it piece by piece, you're shocked that The Calm is all you got that you can depend on. Everything else is gone.

Little boy Juan saw the worst of me. I don't like to think about it, but these last few days, I can't get it out of my head. The feeling of my son, a little boy, coming to see me and hiding behind his mother because I was a bogeyman to him, *El Cucuy*, the scary monster Mexican mothers use to scare children into behaving. I remember the Scooby shoes because his mom bought them for him and I came home looking for money only to find she'd spent it on clothes for the boy. And I said some rotten shit and shook her and all the time Juan watching from the couch, crying so the snot ran out of his nose, not making any noise because he was scared of me.

Maybe it's better if he doesn't remember me. At least the details of what I did. Maybe it's just become an instinct in him to hate me, like an animal that's been burned once and forevermore fears fire. He might not remember the exact moment of being burned, but he knows enough to stay away and mistrust it. I'm that fire.

Last night, I saw the black truck cruise in front of the house. It drove by slowly. He'd followed me, found out where I lived. I prepared myself for a rock being thrown through the window, even a driveby or a Molotov cocktail. I wouldn't blame him. Instead the pickup went by again, just as slowly and then headed down the street and turned right, its red lights disappearing.

I go to the school again. Raquel is right. I need to talk to him, need to tell him the whys and whats of my life, of my mistakes. I need to confess to my boy. If he'll hear me out, maybe he'll understand. I sit in the same place, next to the palm tree grove across from the school. The bell rings, and the students come rolling out in streams, talking excitedly, some running, others pushing and playing. I see Juan come out. He is with the same boys as before. He spots me and says something to his friends. They look in my direction. I am a chimney, smoke drifting out the window into the hot air. It gives me headaches, all this smoking, all this heat, all this waiting. After a bit, Juan crosses the street, but this time his boys stay behind.

His steeltoes kick up dust storms in his wake. He comes over in quick purposeful strides that remind me of a gunslinger in an old western ready to cut down his challenger. Even with the nervousness in my stomach, I'm proud, because I understand that here, in the *barrios*, in Los Duros, you are either victim or warrior. There's no other way of thinking about it. To think about it differently is to already be a victim. It's safer to react and think later, if at all. My boy walks to the side of my truck, where my arm sits on the edge, my hand holding a half-smoked cigarette. He says, "You really my pops?"

"Yes," I say.

"If you're my pops, I gotta tell you, I got no memory of you. My mom never talked about you. She said you were dead and I believed her and it'd be better if you were dead. See, I don't need a pops. I take care of myself and I take care of a lot of other shit. So leave me be. I don't want you around."

"Why don't you get in?" I ask him.

"Aren't you listening, old man? I don't want nothing to do with you."

"Get in and I'll answer some questions for you. You have questions, right?"

"I find my own answers," he says.

"Come on," I say. "You can smoke a cigarette and we can talk things over."

"You know," he says, "my mom is dead. So if you're here to try and get something from her, you're too late."

"That's not what I'm here for."

"So what the fuck is it then?"

"Get in and I'll try to tell you. It's complicated."

"Fuck off, man."

"I want..." and I trail off because I don't know how to say it. After all this time, I feel stupid saying it to him. But I remember Raquel's words to me the other night and I force myself. "I want to make amends," I say.

Juan looks at me and breaks a half-smile, like I just made a stupid joke. "Fuck, man, I don't even know you. For all I know, you're crazy. And even if what you're telling is true, I don't give a damn. You don't have nothing to make amends for. We're strangers, dude."

"I've come a long way," I say, but he cuts me off.

"I don't care if you came from the moon. Just leave me the fuck alone." He turns away and as he passes the front of the truck, he punches the hood with a loud thwack, not hard enough to dent it, but hard enough that he's probably cut a couple of knuckles.

He walks away and when he gets back to his friends, I start the truck and leave. I go home, shut the doors, the windows. I go into the bedroom and pull down the shades. I lie on the mattress and smoke cigarettes all evening long. Raquel calls, but I ignore the phone. Everything's closed in around me and I'm in a cell again. I figure, you can't get away. There's no escape. Prison walls are prison walls and you carry them with you. There's no parole from your life.

§ § §

The knock comes at three in the morning. I know right away it's a cop. Only they knock on your door in the middle of the night. Only they punch at your door with that kind of cocksure authority. My boy's in the squad car. I can see him behind the cop's narrow shoulders, slumped over, looking out the opposite window. The cop, a Chicano, not the worst cop in the world, is telling me that he could have taken Juan in for tagging, but that he's cutting him some slack. "I've got your boy dead to rights, but he's been in trouble before and I know his mom is dead. I'm hoping you've got some sway over the boy. I'd hate to be knocking on your door because he's dead or killed someone. He might be messing around with gangs. I know everyone around here and I'm going to keep an eye out for him. I catch him running around in the middle of the night with spray paint again, you'll be getting a phone call from the station and you'll have a world of trouble on your hands. He gets a break this once."

I thank him and walk out to the car to retrieve Juan. He is sullen, his black T-shirt stretched out at the neck. The cop leaves and Juan stands on the sidewalk looking after the squad car. "Fucking *chota*," he says. "Give a dick a gun and a badge and they can't wait to start messing with you."

"You told him I was your father?"

"He started asking about my parents. I fed him the hard luck story about a dead mother and he asked me where my father was. You can figure out the rest. It was just a way of getting out of a hassle. Didn't mean shit."

"Why don't you come in for a minute?" I ask him.

"What for, so you can give me some advice, like you're really my father?"

"No advice. Just figure you could use a drink or some food. Maybe a ride back to your place. It's a long way."

"I can walk," he says. He puts his hands in his pocket and looks down the dark road.

"You want to walk, I won't stop you," I say.

He takes a long look at me and he says, "Matter of fact, I do want a drink. You need to answer some questions, some real questions."

"I'm right here," I say. "I told you that I'm in Coachella to answer questions."

We walk into the house, Juan, hands still in his jean

pockets, walking behind me at his own crooked pace. I open the door and we go inside. I lead him into the living room where the two lawn chairs sit. It's a blank canvass except for the window where the darkness breaks. The moon is setting.

"You got beer?" he asks.

"I got beer," I say. I come back with a couple of cans. "You been drinking long?" I ask him.

"Long enough to know this is shitty beer," he says popping the tab. He holds it in front of him, studying it, but instead of taking a drink, he turns towards me and says, "Why the hell are you here, man? What do you think you've got to prove anyway?"

"I got things to prove, but mostly to myself. I go out and try and prove them every day."

"And what is that?"

"That I can walk a free man, stay a free man, that I can live in this world another day without it taking what I've got left, which isn't a lot."

"I can see that," he says looking around the empty room. "I've got more shit in my trailer, dude. It's so funny it's sad."

"You're right about that," I say taking a drink. "So you've got questions."

"Yeah, I got questions," he says. He still hasn't taken a swig from the beer he is holding. "Like where the fuck you been? How come you haven't ever bothered to drop a line, make a call? Where the hell were you when my mom died? Why are you a two-bit junkie? Why aren't you dead? Questions like that." His hand tightens around the can, so that beer leaks down the side and onto the floor. He keeps his eyes on me.

"I've been in jail," I say steadily. "Ten years and then another year living in Chualar picking grapes and doing odd jobs so that I could come out here and find you."

"You don't think I remember?" he says. "You don't think I remember you punching my mother around? Huh? You got an answer for that?"

"There's no answer for that," I say quietly. But that isn't enough, so I try. "I was a junkie," I say. "A lowdown, mean junkie that didn't care about a goddamn thing except getting high. I did things I would have punched someone in the jaw for saying I was capable of doing. I did lots worse things to your mom than hit her. I destroyed her faith in me and in God, probably. I screwed up your life, let you down, got myself locked up, handed my family over to the cruelties of this cold world. That's no real answer, I don't think, but it's the truth."

"You don't know the half of it," he says. "You can't even begin to know what you did to us, motherfucker. You think you can come out here and make things right? You want to confess, you go talk to a priest. You save that shit for someone else." He takes a long drink of the beer.

"I know it's been hard for you," I say.

"Hard," he says sharply. "Hard? Hey, man, when you left, my mom moved us out here to Los Duros and it wasn't long before she took up with some drunk motherfucker. You know what he did to me?" he says. He stands, pulling up his T-shirt. There are burn scars along his stomach and going around his skinny ribs. "You want to know the sick shit he did to me when I was nine? While you were sucking shit in a prison cause you couldn't control your junkie ass, a fucking pervert was sucking my dick one night and burning me the next."

It hits me, the nausea, like I'm going to vomit up the self-hate that's churning up my soul. I stand up, try to move towards him, because I want to grab hold of him and try and squeeze out the pain, to take it into my body, to have him give it to me, the hatred and anger, the sorrow and disgrace. But Juan backs up quickly. "Don't touch me, *puto*," he says. And I can see in the dim light that he's crying, his body trying hard to hold back the shakes. "I don't want nothing from you, man." And he throws the half-full beer at the blank wall. He takes off towards the front door. I follow him, saying, "Juan, *espérate!*" But he doesn't. He pulls the door open wildly, and takes off into the dark, his hands back in his pockets.

By the time I find the keys to the truck and take off after him, he's gone.

§ § §

"He was saying that illegals bring leprosy, that they are massacring the youth of America, that it's a disgrace that they haven't been rounded up, arrested, hounded from their homes. Drug dealers and thugs, speaking a foreign tongue, invaders from the south, enacting a *Reconquista*," Raquel is telling Leo when I come in the next morning. Leo listens, an eyebrow hitched, a smirk on his face like he doesn't take it seriously.

"They always say those things, Raquel. That's what they do. There's an election coming and the *gabachos* always start screaming about the Mexicans."

"No, not like this," she says. "Not like this. This man wasn't playing to the crowd. He was serious, full of hatred and anger. I was afraid."

"How many where there?" asks Leo.

"I don't know. A lot and most of them nodding and agreeing with him. His people gave out pamphlets and signed people up for the Citizens Watch Group. He said that if the government didn't crack down on the Mexicans, then Americans would."

Leo scratches his chin, and taking his cowboy hat, turns to me. "Don't tell me you're afraid of the Minute Men too."

"I don't know anything about that," I say. I almost didn't come to work today. I need to find Juan, but sitting at the entrance of Los Duros all night hasn't done any good. There's no sign of him.

"They're for real," Raquel says. "We should organize a peaceful march from the church to the park, a family event where we can show the community that we won't be made afraid. Don't you think, Juan?"

I fiddle around at the front desk, making like I'm looking for the keys to the van. "I gotta make my pickups," I say.

Leo stops me. "Hey, no shower runs today. I need you to pick up Henry. He's at the house. Bring him here. I'll get one of the guys to make your rounds this morning." I nod and walk out, Raquel looking after me with confusion.

She follows me outside, where I'm lighting a cigarette before I step into the van. "You alright?" she asks.

"Fine," I say.

"You don't seem fine. Did something happen with your son?"

"Gotta go," I say, and I get into the van and leave.

Henry's waiting outside. He's in his chair, smoking, an old red bandana tied around his forehead. It's only nine a.m. and it's already almost a hundred degrees. He gives me a wave and rolls to the gate, cig dangling from his lips. His face is shaved, his hair freshly cut. He's in a better mood than when I last saw him. I come around and give him a nod. "You ready to roll?" I ask.

"Always ready to roll, *culero*," he says smiling as he pats the wheels of his chair.

"Didn't mean it like that," I say.

"No worries, *vato*. I can take a joke, even God's jokes." I help him into the van and pack his chair in the back. When I get in, he says, "Got a job, Juan. They're putting me to use at the school. I'm going to help out the new teacher down there, some *vato* from Texas who is teaching the kids about videos and music and computers."

"That's good," I say.

"Yeah, man. I learned computers in the army, bro. They managed to teach a Mexican a thing or three besides killing. They're not paying me too much *feria*, that's for sure, but it makes a body feel good to know he's got something to do except go to doctor's appointments and drink BudLite all day."

"Yeah, that's good," I say.

"What's wrong with you this fine morning?"

"*Nada.*"

"Don't seem like *nada*. Seems *como algo*." He looks at me, his eyes searching the side of my face, making me feel uncomfortable. "My old man giving you a hard time?" When I don't say anything, he faces the front again. "Don't want to talk? That's cool. I'm in a good mood, dude. A damned good mood." He starts singing, *"Si te dicen que yo vivo en las cantinas."*

"Listen," I say all of the sudden, even before I know what I'm doing. "I had a bad night and I'm having a bad day, so cool it. I just want to do my job, keep my mouth shut and don't want no one fucking with me."

Henry looks at me, the song dying, his eyes squinting like his father's. "Yeah, man, I can tell." But he lets it drop and we drive to the Center in silence. The whole time I watch the side of the road, even though I know I won't see him.

When we get to the Center, Raquel is on the phone. She's calling people up, organizing. Leo's jumped on board, hearing from the mayor's office that the stage is being set to bring in a presidential candidate to Palm Springs who's planning a fund raiser and a hardcore anti-immigrant speech.

"Why here?" Henry asks.

"It's about the *L.A. Times* writing that article on Los Duros last year," Leo says. "About the illegal dumping and the burning of the toxic waste. Kids with cancer and lung disease make people ask questions even if the sick kids are brown. Lots of money involved in dumping out here. So instead of cleaning the shit up, they've decided to distract the good people of Palm Springs by blaming our kids for everything from leprosy to embezzlement."

"No shit," Henry says.

"That's right, no shit. It's going to get a lot hotter, too. This is a perfect spot for using our kids to raise money from these rich folks. You waltz in, talk about drugs and illegals gumming up the system. You get the millionaires wagging their heads and writing big campaign donations. It happens every time, but this year it'll be different. Lots more news coverage, and probably a lot of right-wingers coming in to cash in on the hatred they've drummed up."

"Let's make sure they don't," says Henry. "People around here may not give too much a damn about themselves, but they won't let their kids get spit on."

The march is led by kids, most of them from the high school in Thermal. Lot's of parents are scared. There's been rumors that ICE will be lurking around ready to throw a net around people who even look illegal. But the kids, many of them born in the U.S., aren't afraid. They want to be heard. Men are threatening their parents with deportation, men who don't know anything about them or their lives. Men who sweep into their towns claiming that they have a say over them, over their homes and parents. Los Duros isn't much. To an outsider it's no more than a third world hell hole with dust for streets, skinny stray dogs, and hundreds of shanties and hovels. But to the kids, Los Duros, Thermal, and Mecca are home and these men are laying claim to them. There's a couple of hundred kids set up in front of the high school. Henry, Leo, and Raquel have rallied adults, citizens, to show up with signs and banners. Raquel told people not to bring Mexican flags. "We want to assert our citizenship in America." But few listened. The Mexican flag is everywhere, painted on signs and T-shirts. People wave small ones and big ones. Those with bullhorns shout out their slogans and songs in Spanish. They won't be told that they have to be ashamed of their families, their heritage, their skin.

There's a news camera or two, with reporters standing on the sidelines recording as the mass of people march into the street and walk towards the courthouse in Coachella. It's a hot day, too hot to be taking a long march. But those with water share it. Parents carry small children and everyone seems strengthened and determined by the meaning of it. I stand next to Henry, who wears a T-shirt, sleeves cut away, sporting a picture of Zapata in full revolutionary gear. He has his Purple Heart and some other ribbons pinned to the shirt.

He says, "I wake up every goddamn day wondering why the hell I gave up my legs, why I got sent to the desert to come back with two stumps. And then on a day like this." He trails off like the idea has faded so he can't remember it like he wants.

Standing behind him, I look down at his stumps. Both above the knee. It doesn't seem like there's anything worth that. Not these marches. They aren't going to change anything. He knows that even if he can't say it.

"Let's get in there," he says. And he pushes into the crowd. I walk next to him. The marchers chant, "*Nosotros somos Americanos*" and "No human is illegal!" The Center arranged a parade permit, and police stand on the side of the road watching. They wear helmets with face guards. A line of them holds shields and batons ready. It's like the moment leading up to a prison riot. The heat of the day is up, and you can feel the people's anger at the sight of the cops. There's a pressure building up, like everyone holding their breath until they have to exhale or burst. It isn't going to take much. Someone throwing something, a push, a curse word, a clumsy punch.

But the cops are only the mask of what people are angry at. The real thing lies behind the mask and is nowhere near the march. Will never be near. The power behind the mask doesn't get its hands dirty. It doesn't get near enough to feel the heat come up through the asphalt, right through the people, the hot day reflecting their anger. It's all pointless because you can strike at that mask as hard as you can, but you'll never hit the face of power behind it. It can't be touched. But it can hit you. The cops on the street are there to remind everyone of that. So what good does it do to fight?

A girl yells into a bullhorn: "The people are tired of being blamed for every problem. We're tired of being kicked around and moved at will. We're tired of the poverty, of the police, of ICE! We deserve respect. We are humans!"

As we get closer to the courthouse, there are more cameras and a reporter with a microphone spots Henry. He walks up to us. "Hey, you a veteran?" he asks.

"Yeah, I'm a veteran," Henry says looking up at the man's face.

"Can I interview you? I just want to ask you some

questions about why you're here and what these people want."

"Ain't it obvious?" Henry asks. "Look around, *vato*, these are poor people. They are forgotten until goddamned politicians come in here to stir up all these rich folk. Tell them we're thieves and criminals. They make a lot of noise, make it harder for us to feed our children, to live in peace. Our people want the same thing you want. To be left alone to work and live."

"How'd you get injured?" the reporter asks.

"Making sure you get to do your job."

"No, really," he says.

"An IED that some other brown bastard planted in the dirt because he didn't want us there."

"Is that the way you see it?" the reporter asks.

"Damn right," Henry says. "Any other way of seeing it?"

"Maybe," he says.

"Maybe for you," Henry says. "But all I see is big money rolling in, buying and taking what it wants, kicking people off land, and using them like pieces of equipment, no more important than cheap tractors, the same way they do over there."

"In Iraq?"

"Yeah, Iraq. Tons of poor people who don't know whether to shit, run, or lay down and die. This country's solution is always to shoot first and ask questions later."

"Is this a peace rally too?" he asks.

"No peace over here unless there's peace over there," Henry says.

The reporter smiles. "Who is that on your shirt?"

"Emiliano Zapata."

"Who is that?"

"A revolutionary. Even you should know that," Henry answers. "Aren't you Mexican?"

"Not me," he says. "I'm American."

"You saying I'm not?" Henry says, his eyes on the reporter's face looking for any reason to jump at him.

I push in front of the reporter.

"Hey, you got the answers you want. Now get the hell out of here before this guy wastes you."

"It's all right," Henry says. "I can handle myself."

The reporter keeps smiling but he walks away towards the sidewalk where four of five people are standing with anti-immigrant signs. They wave American flags, their faces red in the heat as they shout, "Go Back Home! No Amnesty!"

And then I hear something from up front, a commotion, someone yelling and then someone yelling back, then a few voices, some of them angry, others scared. Someone has thrown something or spit on someone, who knows? There's shoving and the line collapses around a fight, people shoving and cursing, at least until the cops get involved, and then they spring on the crowd, swinging their sticks wild, cracking heads and shoulders and faces. People push to move forward into the action while those that are closest to the violence, push back to move away, to get out of the circle where the police are busting heads. I don't know who started what, but I know who's going to finish it. So I grab the back of Henry's chair and pull him in the opposite direction. "What are you doing, *vato*?" he yells. But I keep pulling him away as the scene gets wilder. People are getting knocked to the hot pavement, and more police mill around swinging their sticks at whatever head happens to be nearby. I see a camera tripod go down, the crowd stomping the machine to bits. And this was going to help who?

I've seen enough to know who wins these things. It isn't the Mexicans. So I pull Henry out of the scrap even though he's yelling at me to stop. I turn the corner, heading for the van. "What the hell are you doing?" Henry keeps yelling. I don't say anything until we get back. "Hey, man, I'm on parole. I don't need this kind of trouble," I say. "This ain't got nothing to do with you. I'm not going back to the slam for anybody."

Henry shakes his head, his eyes full of scorn. "Hey, Juan, you wanna split, you split but I need to stay. There's things more important than your shit. We're trying to make a statement out here, and you run at the first sign of trouble."

"Get in the van, Henry. We don't have time for this *pedo*. I'm not going to argue with you."

He does what I tell him, pulling himself into the passenger seat leaving his wheelchair empty. I fold it up and put it in the back and walk around to the driver's side. I light a cigarette and climb in. Henry looks out his window, too angry to talk. I let him be. After a few miles, he says, "You aren't the only one with something to lose. There's a lot of people out here that are putting their lives at risk, their families, everything, on the line."

"Well, that's their choice," I say. "I have to make my choice. I have to live with it."

"That's a narrow attitude," he says.

"Call it what you want, Henry. I spent ten years thinking about my plan. I'm not going to let anyone mess it up."

"Don't tell me about your prison plans," Henry says. "I'm in prison till I die. So you ain't got shit to say to me about that."

"You're right," I say. "There isn't no man who can tell another man about his prison. And there ain't no man who can get another out of that prison house either."

I let that sit. The truth is only you can pick how you're going to do your time. I'm not going to throw away my last chance for some doomed protest that isn't going to change anything. Best you can do is keep your head down, try to keep from letting the worst of the blows do too much damage. Maybe there'll be enough of you left to find something that you can still save, make yours. If you're that lucky, protect it.

We're quiet the rest of the way to Henry's house. Maybe he's thinking about his legs. About how they're bits of flesh and bone mixed in with the sand thousands of miles away. I hurt for him. I hurt for Juan and his friends, for the *mojados* I drive to the showers, those working and fighting out there in the heat trying to believe that what they think, say, or do means a goddamn thing.

§ § §

I didn't go in the next day. I spent the night parked outside Juan's trailer. I didn't see the peacock at first. I was fighting the sleep, cigarette after cigarette, thinking about where it had all gone to shit. Why I'd made the goddamn decisions I'd made, whether or not they even were decisions. It's a cop out, yes, to fool yourself into thinking that things only happen to you, but there's more to it than that. Because there's no set of rules. No one tells you the score when you're born. You learn it a little at a time and for *pendejos* like me, it's too late by the time you learn.

I was thinking all these things when I heard him screech. He was practically in my ear, mad that I wasn't paying attention to him. He was blue with a little crown of inky flowers making a Mohawk on his head. His squawks froze me. I stared at him and he stared back. He was beautiful, proud. It made me feel good for a minute, because he was here, and maybe it was a sign that I was supposed to be here too. I watched him quietly, trying to memorize what he looked like.

Finally, he walked away. I wondered whose he was and how an animal like him could be here, of all places. He belonged in a fairy story, in a myth. I wished Juan were there for me to point the bird out to him, for me to make some kind of connection to the peacock. Because this was significant, wasn't it? This was magic. It was a sign, even if there was nobody to see it but me.

2.

I won't lie. I came out here because of a girl. A friend of a friend from San Antonio, my hometown. I met Gloria at a dirty-dirty south side party. She was smart, a college girl with plans, good to talk to, pretty, too pretty for me. But I've got lots of personality so we got to dating. She was studying to be a teacher. I'd just dropped out of college--didn't know what I wanted to do--but was reading a lot, making small change setting up websites for friends' bands, spinning at parties, messing around, but waiting for an opportunity. When Gloria got a job in Thermal, California, I followed her up even though she didn't ask me to. I thought she was the right girl or something like that.

I let the principal at her school know I was a digital media wiz and that's how I landed at Desert Mirage High School teaching the vocational students about computers even though I didn't have a degree. The school figured, it's only poor Mexicans he's teaching, so no sweat on the credentials. Gloria left after only six months, burnt out, ready to make some more money in Burbank where more kids speak English. I thought about moving with her, but I stayed. I'm still not a hundred percent sure why, but part of the reason was because this place started to make sense to me. I began to think that maybe I belonged out here with the burnouts, the *rancheros*, the *cholitos*, the *indios*, the *mojados*. The kids no one around here really gives a damn about. There came a day when I realized I gave a damn about them and I didn't want to stop.

Gloria had already told me she was leaving and I was thinking about my next move. It was this one kid, a Tarascan Indian, who made me realize I wasn't following my girl out of this place. I spotted him sitting outside the principal's office. He was sitting on one of those small plastic chairs, his T-shirt worn thin, but clean enough. His face was pockmarked all over. He was a big boy, fat and tall like me. He was trying to make himself look small so no one would notice him. I nodded at him. He wouldn't look me in the eye. He had jumpy hands. I knew this kid. I'd grown up with him, been him.

A couple of hours later, I walked through the office again and he was still sitting in the same place, still staring at his jumpy hands. I asked the secretary what the deal was. "He won't write an apology to his teacher for throwing his desk over." So I walked up to him and asked him what the problem was. The kid looked at me like I was speaking Japanese. I asked him his name in Spanish and he said, "Tarasco." The kid didn't really understand. No one had bothered to figure that out. That happens a lot around here.

I asked Principal Joe to put him in my class. No one wants to deal with the Tarascans. They mostly speak P'urhépecha. The other kids make fun of them. They call them *chacas*, after Michoacán, the state in Mexico where they are from. The teachers don't know what to do with them so they sit around not doing anything much.

My class is the designated spot for the troublemakers and dummies. That's the way they do out here. No one's got time for the throwaways. You've got thirty kids in class, most of them already way behind, and then you throw in a Tarascan or two? Most of these teachers already think they're Mother Teresa, working with the migrants, the undocumented, the poor, you know, the Unteachables. For a lot of them, the job is nothing but a paycheck and maybe some easy self-satisfaction. They leave Mecca and Thermal in Priuses and SUVs to houses in Indio and Cathedral City far from this reality. Not me. I live in Thermal in a trailer just like the kids.

It was Tarasco who made me see that my destiny lay out here. I'd never thought I had a destiny. It's a crazy word, a crazy idea for a scraggy-bearded, long-haired, tall, fatboy Mexican pirate like me. But there you go. Faster than I knew it, I got to thinking about them as my kids. I wanted to kick it with them, teach them what they already knew but were told they didn't or shouldn't know. I got to wanting to write poetry in their minds, to lead them into bringing some light in the dark desert of endless sun. Poetry. Only, they were the real poets. You have to be one uninterested individual not to see that. You have to be one uninterested individual for these kids not to love you.

Believe me, I didn't get here a Tecumseh or a Zapata teaching revolution in front of a desk. I got here a *chueco*, smoking bowlfuls of prime green, in love with a girl whose face I barely remember anymore. Day one it was way too hot to sleep in my trailer and my girl didn't want a live-in boyfriend. It was official when she said, "You're so big and my apartment is so small." So I'd go sleep at the school. I'd drive to my air-conditioned classroom and crash out on the floor making sure to get up before the janitors came in.

The desert has a crazy sharp learning curve, like falling-off-a-cliff sharp. I felt dizzy, discombobulated, always hot, out of place, wondering why I'd ever left San Antonio. But it started to make me see things differently. The kids here were just like me. They were visitors too. This fancy school wasn't for them. The learning wasn't for them. They were just placeholders till the big houses with the rich families crept up and pushed them out.

Their scared parents tell them to keep their mouths shut and heads down for fear that they'll draw attention and be deported or arrested. Teachers too. Just about every adult around here conveys a central lesson: it's your fate to be a slave. I couldn't teach them that. "Don't buy that mess," I told them. "We've got to make them see us. To make them hear us." They wanted to know, how we going to do that? "We have everything we need in this classroom," I told them. "We have brains, we got know how, we got creativity, most of all, we got *ganas*. You know what *ganas* is? That's determination and inspiration." I tell them that we're going to have to learn from each other, inspire each other.

"You only get one shot in this world, one life, one chance. Why spend it on your knees? Living in fear of the good citizens of America? Don't stay in the shadows suffering quiet like they tell you you have to." I tell them just like that. I keep it basic. I remind them, they remind me. That's our pact.

My father taught me that you need some luck in this life, but not even luck will work if you don't have *ganas*. He got up every day of his life at five in the morning to work on long haul rigs at a shop on the south side. Did it until he fell over dead one fine morning. Right from the top of a rig. Lost his balance when he started bleeding out from cirrhosis. He was only 53. But he never did take shit that I saw. He didn't give it either. He went about his business and always told it like it was. When I was a kid, he'd say, "Guillermo, keep your head down, your elbows moving, your ass in gear."

The only time I ever saw him get mad was when some manager put the whole shift in a room and accused the bunch of them of stealing tools. Me and my mom were picking him up from work and we were waiting on him. My pop was clockwork, so when he didn't come out for a while, my mom sent me out to see what was taking so long. I liked going up to the office because it gave me a chance to walk through the main yard with the dozens of semi tractors and bobtails like sleeping steel elephants and iron whales. Through the window I could see my pop and some other workers, a couple I recognized as his pals, sitting while boss man waved his arms and yelled. He was saying, "That goddamn combo kit didn't walk off on its own. And every one of you sonsabitches are staying put till someone tells me something about it." So with everyone watching boss man, my pop stood up and said, "I've been called a son of a bitch plenty of times, but I'll be damned if I sit here off the clock to be called a thief." And he walked out of there with boss man looking after him with his mouth opened stupid.

I got my chops from my old man. I've never been able to shut my mouth if you try to get over on someone I love. It's unfairness that really gets to me. I'll call you on it. I have to.

It didn't take long to understand how it works around Mirage High, the nakedness of it, right out in the open for anyone to see, only no one seems to want to say it. And yet everyone knows it, but it's like everyone agrees silently to play by crooked rules. It was Tarasco that made me decide that I wasn't going to stay quiet while everyone conspired to get over on my kids. Just before she left, my girl asked me, "Just what do you think you're going to do, Guillermo? It's no use." I told her, "I'm going to do everything and anything I can to change it."

"You're just going to get yourself in trouble. You're going to get them in trouble." She didn't see that there was already trouble, so much trouble that she was cutting out for safer ground. "Maybe you like trouble," she told me the last time I talked to her. "Well, I don't run from it." She hung up.

It was easy to get Tarasco assigned to my class. No one really cared what happened to him. He was destined to fall through the cracks. The system depends on it. No one notices the loss of a poor, illiterate illegal. The more of them that drop out, flunk out, or get tossed out, the better. This school, it's beautiful. A multimillion-dollar facility with shiny new buildings, computers, and manicured lawns. But it's for the upper middle-class kids that will start to move into Thermal and Coachella and Mecca when the new suburbs start filling up. That means bye-bye Mexicans. These kids are only short-term tenants. They're migrants just passing through until the Owners show up. And they'll show up. You can't drive the 1111 highway that connects Palm Springs, Rancho Mirage, Cathedral City, Indio and all the rest of the desert cities without passing 30 or 40 country clubs. And all of them with Spanish names. The walls are built high to keep out the riffraff and protect the rich golfers who swing away at little balls oblivious to everything outside the fieldstone parameter.

Stick around for all of two minutes and you'll notice the groundskeepers, short, thick brown men pulling tools and hoses, clipping plants, making sure everything stays in pristine condition for the Owners. Drive back to Mecca and you'll see where the peasants live. The *peones* of the 21st century. The broken down houses, the families living in cars or hovels, the *colonias* like Los Duros where the kids resemble the children of late night CARE commercials more than the suburban kids living in the high class "desert communities."

I tell the kids, "You're too smart not to get a handle on this. The rich need migrants, they need the workers, and they need them to be disposable, to be quiet, to eat it and not complain too loudly." I want them to learn that they have to say hell no to that. So I teach more than computers. I teach them our history. Encourage them to hang on to their language, their past, their ancestors. "That's your legacy. That means it's yours, hard earned, special. The Aztecs, Toltecs, Mayans, the revolutionaries of the past, the Cesar Chavezes, the Dolores Huertas. But it's fragile, easy to steal. They'll take everything from you if they can. Family, home, livelihood, dreams, health, dignity, history, your past and your present."

In the beginning it was almost like talking to myself, convincing myself that what I was seeing was real and that to live in it and do nothing would mean something terrible. I don't know anything about revolutions or protests. Where I'm from, you're taught that complaining is a waste of time. Activism is a foreign concept. Even my pop hated the *La Raza* stuff. He didn't have time for that. He used to say they were bums and hippies. For us, it was all about just keep on keeping on.

But that's not possible in this desert. It's a survival issue here. I got the idea when I was using my cell to video my new digs to my mom back in San Antonio. I got the kids to say a few things about themselves in the classroom. My mom told me that they were sweet. "*Los pobrecitos, tan chulitos!*" she said. And I thought, why not get them to film their lives, tell their own stories? What could be better than that for opening their eyes, and maybe even other people's eyes?

I told Principal Joe first. "We're going to make movies. All I need is a couple of digital cameras. Some software. We've already got computers. We'll set up a website. They'll learn all sorts of skills. It's a good idea, right?"

He wasn't buying it. "They'll wind up making inappropriate material. Equipment will go missing or get broken."

I convinced him though. I told him I'd be the bad cop, make sure they weren't filming cockfights or whatever it was he was worried about. I kept at it till he gave me the go-ahead, $500 bucks, enough to get two cameras that were half decent. I unpacked them in front of the kids for full effect. "These are for you," I told them. "We're going to make movies. We're going to shoot them on these digital cameras. We're going to set up a website so that people can see what's up around here. You have a voice and now you've got a good way of getting heard."

The kids weren't all that clear on the concept, although I caught Tarasco smiling. So we spent the day talking about ideas. A lot of their ideas sounded like MTV reality junk. But I was psyched because the more we talked, they started to get excited about the possibilities. They had plenty of things to say. They had ideas about what they wanted to change. We got to convincing each other that we could change things. And they will change things. I wouldn't be here if I didn't believe it.

§ § §

Los Duros is right out of one of those late night help the children in South America commercials, hovels sweltering in the heat, sand and grit blowing in the wind, open sewers and filth. The dump is right there, within eyesight of the *colonia*. The kids ride their bikes past it. They walk by it every morning and night. They play in the runoff, bare feet and legs crusted with toxic slime. The Indians who own the reservation make big bucks letting the construction companies dump their poisons there. Paints, chemicals, asbestos tiles, old wiring, stuff that should be shot out into space, not made into a playground. The junk piles up everyday until the weekend comes and then the Indians pay a couple of the migrants to set fire to the mess and it burns all day and night long. The smoke settles down on Los Duros like a fog from hell making the kids sick with asthmas and cancers. The toxic gunk gets in the water supply, making its way to the Salton Sea where it blends with all the other pesticides and pollutants that kills the fish and birds, and later, the people. But no one seems to give a damn. After all, it's only illegals breathing it. Who cares? If they don't like it, they can go back where they come from.

María, one of my kids, a 14-year old girl, has some kind of leukemia. She's always pale, always tired, misses school all the time. When she gets real bad, they see her at the county hospital. But there's no money for serious treatment. The cancer could have come from anywhere. Except, everyone around here knows it's the poisons. María's the one who told me about the dump first. I asked for ideas and she said, "You should come to Los Duros." I showed up with a couple of the other teachers from the school to check it out. They'd both been teaching at the school for a couple of years, young committed types, but they'd never ventured into Duros.

We parked on the dirt road and got out, walking slowly towards the dump. It was overgrown, stinking of burned rubber and other things I couldn't put my finger on. It looked like Mount Doom, alive, belching out its sickness for people to breathe. Three men with bandanas over their mouths and noses, poured gasoline over a huge pile of debris, each of them swinging five gallon cans gushing streams of amber until all the containers were empty. Then one of them struck a match, and throwing it on the pile hauled ass over to where the other two stood watching. He almost got his *nalgas* burned out. The pile went up like a car explosion right out of a *Die Hard* movie, a wall of flame near invisible in the bright sun. It was the smoke that made its impression, covering the sky like black squid ink spreading in water. The three workers stood there for a minute until the heat and the smoke drove them away from the flaming mountain of garbage.

We stood there watching like statues. None of us had ever seen anything like it. Pyromaniacs hadn't seen anything like it. And all I could think was, this is what the kids need to show. Life in hell.

Because people couldn't know about this or it wouldn't be happening. All we had to do was show them and they'd be shocked, outraged, pissed. I took some pictures and the other two teachers started to get nervous. "It's disgusting," one of them said making it clear that she wanted to split. "Yeah," the other one said, "but do you think you ought to be taking pictures? They won't like it."

"Who won't like it?" I said.

"The Indians who own this spot. They don't like strangers coming in here and they sure wouldn't want someone taking pictures of illegal activities."

"Don't be a *panocha*," I told him. He was a young guy, maybe a couple of years older than me, if that, and he didn't like being called out.

"Don't be stupid," he said. "Let's get out of here before there's trouble."

"I'll put the camera away, but let's walk around a little. Talk to some people," I said.

They didn't like it, but it was better than standing around at a crime scene. So we found María's house. It was an old, sagging shack, paint peeling like dried bark, a few dingy windows, a couple covered with cardboard. The screen door hung open like a dead dog's mouth, a broken metal mess clinging to one rusty hinge. I knocked on the door and waited. No one came out. Instead, the sheet that covered the front window moved a little. Classic move to see what bill-collecting asshole or warrant-holding cop was at the door.

"*¿Quién es?*"

"*Buenas tardes. Soy el maestro de María. Estamos visitando a los padres de nuestros estudiantes.*"

The door opened slowly and an old woman, in her late hundreds, peeked through the crack.

"*¿De la escuela?*"

"*Sí.* I teach María."

The old woman opened the door wide and told me María was in bed. "She sick."

"I don't want to bother her. I just wanted to let you know I'm her teacher. If you need anything, you should tell María to let me know." The old woman, her brown skin wrinkled and parched, her few strands of gray hair pulled back into a threadbare bun, looked at me suspiciously. She knitted her brow thinking hard for English words. "We need nothing," she said slowly. From behind, I could see a little girl trying to get a look at me.

"Okay," I said. "I'm here to help. Your granddaughter is

very smart. I know she's sick, so if you needs something, a ride to the doctor, or to school. Whatever, *no más dígame*."

"No phone," she said.

María came into the room. She looked bad, worn out, her face even more pale than I normally saw in the classroom. She wore a T-shirt with the school name on it and dirty *chanclas*. Her nose was running.

"Hello, Sir," she said. I could tell she was embarrassed. "What are you doing here?"

"Just getting a look at the neighborhood. I thought I'd drop in and see what's up." The old woman left the door and went back into another room. Now at the door, María said, "You can come in, but it's not very nice in here."

"I don't want to bother you. Your grandma said you were sick. You live here with her?"

"My mom too. That's my sister, Juana," she said putting her hand on the little girl's head. Juana smiled, a couple of teeth missing, her brown eyes squinted in a silly kid grin. "My mom's working."

"Well, get some rest," I told her. "I was just here to check out the place and I thought I'd say hello. Let me know if you need anything." She smiled and said thanks and I left feeling useless because of course she needed help. She needed to be in a place with real medical care, a place that had a clean bed. The teachers got into my truck and we headed out like tourists.

Near the gate, I saw Tarasco. He was on a bike, following behind us half hidden by the dust in our wake. He was the bulkiest *vato* by far, his mop of black hair a dead giveaway. I slowed down the truck and rolled the window down, motioning him over with my hand.

"What you doing? Spying on us?" I asked him.

He smiled an accident of a smile. He waved and turned back on the dirt trail without saying a word. The kid was *más indio que la chingada.*

§ § §

A routine traffic stop, only there's nothing routine about it. A cop, needing to make his monthly quota, spots a beat up old Cutlass, windows rolled down because the air conditioning doesn't work. The muffler's for shit, banging and smoking like an old cigarette fiend. Pulls it over. There's a woman at the wheel, nervous as hell. There's a girl, scared and quiet. Even though he could give the woman a citation and let it go at that, he's feeling like a hero and he calls ICE. He holds the car, waiting for the men in blue to get there. The highway carries drugs, guns, humans, and god knows what else. The decision has been made. The woman and kid have got to go. The ICE men walk up, question them on the side of the road. They want papers. Only the girl has anything, a school ID with her smiling like she belongs. They order them into the back of a van. It's back to Mexico for them. It doesn't matter that the girl has leukemia. That's her tough luck. Lots of tough luck stories in the desert. They're just doing their job.

Things like this make me want to burn the world down with a match. Just strike it and let it all go to hell like the toxic dump in Duros. Because really, who would suffer? Not so much the spit on, the illegals, the poor, the young, the old, and the dying. They're lost already. It would be the oblivious middle class and the carefree wealthy that'd suffer for a change. I'm starting to see this place with Mississippi Eyes. It's got me turning.

And so María is gone just like that. Picked up because her mom's jalopy was a smoking mess and the cop who stopped her was doing his sworn duty. The wheels grind like that everyday. Some poor sucker, some chump with no name, gets ground under and no one cares.

That's how I get into the smuggling business. The old woman, María's *abuelita*, shows up at the school. God knows how she found me, or how she got here. But she tells me, "They took them away. Help them." For a $1000 I can get her and her mother back here. A few phone calls, a couple of loans, a drive to Mexicali, and I bring them home. The word spreads, and just like that, I've got street cred with my students. Not bad.

§ § §

Tarasco is a lost cause, or so his first teacher tells me, the one he freaked out by throwing his desk over. Every morning, Tarasco, the boy-giant of Los Duros, creeps like a cat into the classroom. He doesn't want to be seen. He doesn't make eye contact, doesn't speak. He's mortified when caught in my gaze, a paralyzed *chaca*, one vulnerable alien. At first, I think it's an Indian thing, the silent stoic figure, noble and whatever. But there's plenty of Tarascan kids running around, and they're not all quiet or noble. This kid doesn't know what to do with himself. "You're too big to be shy," I tell him. "You might as well own your size." He only turns red and looks at the wall.

The other students cut up, the girls flirting because it's their only way out, the boys pretending to be tough because the only other choice is suicide. They're kids, lonely and confused, but that's not allowed here. They work with their parents in the field, come to school when they can, hope, like all kids, that their lives are going to be better. Hell if I know how. I watch Tarasco because even behind his mask of diffidence, I see something alive and fierce in his eyes. I don't want him to drown like I almost did, don't want him to bleed to death on a stricken street, calling for his mother as cars pass by without even slowing down. Mostly, I don't want what I see in his eyes to fade out into nothing.

I tell my kids we have a mission. "Los Duros is a sick place, a place sickened by greed and it goes on because no one sees it but you. We can't let them get away with choking you to death, so we're going to make a film. We're going to record them in the act. We're going to show the poison seeping into the ground and into the water. If people see it, maybe they'll care." The kids are psyched, ready to roll out and use their cameras. Maybe the revolution will be televised.

Principal Joe, an old school Chicano from the days when Cesar had them striking out here, the *huelgas*, the teamsters cracking migrant heads, the UFW holding strong—is supportive of the project in his quiet way. But he runs a tight ship and he's got to answer to a school board, to supervisors, all those sell-outs and paper pushers who don't give a damn about the school so long as it keeps the kids off the streets.

"So how's the documentary going?" Principal Joe

squints his eyes as he watches the students milling around for lunch outside. It's a hot day, but you wouldn't know it from the way the students goof around. Principal Joe is small, a short, dark *mestizo* with a gray bushy mustache and a straw cowboy hat.

"It's progressing. The kids are into it. They're learning a lot."

"I think it's a good idea. But it's going to get you some pushback. I know these people. There's money involved in this thing and money is always serious."

"We're serious too."

"I can see that," he says and he walks over to talk to a group of boys.

The other teachers don't think it will work. It's nothing too overt. But always these patronizing questions about The Project, and wondering about whether the kids are up to it. But they'll see.

Tarasco picks things up quick. He doesn't say much. He watches and learns. Before long, other kids ask him for help. He never refuses, just walks over and peers at the computer screen like he's looking into its digital soul. He fiddles around while the other kids look on as he fixes the problem. They say thanks, and he nods, but says nothing. He goes back to his station and picks up his work again.

"What you got?" I ask him.

He points at the screen. There are some still shots of Los Duros at twilight. The dust in the air helps to diffuse the light, giving everything—the dirt streets, the broken down houses, the shoeless children, and the palm trees—a kind of sad grace that I couldn't see when I was there.

"Damn, it almost looks beautiful," I tell him. He doesn't look at me. Just watches the screen till I walk away. Every day after school, he sticks around with a few of the others. They want to record lyrics to a rap they're writing about Thermal. Tarasco just wants to keep fiddling with his pictures. He wants to learn the sound-mixing program, the film-editing program, the web builder. I tell him he can stick around as late as he wants. I tell them all that. I figure as long as they're here doing their thing, they're not out there.

This one student, Oscar, who I figured right away for a gangster, brings in his friend, a skinny kid named Juan. He watches them screw around with a small soundboard as they try and lay down some lyrics. He doesn't say much to them, but it's obvious that they look for his approval.

"You interested in this stuff?" I ask him as he sits on a desk watching.

He shrugs. "Yeah. It's cool." He's wiry and short. He has restless eyes. They betray intelligence and a kind of anxious weariness. He's too young for those eyes.

"You should sign up for my class then, learn it all from the ground up."

"I don't think they'll let me," he says.

"Why not?"

"Too much trouble. They kicked me out for two weeks and they put me in all the dumb-ass classes."

"Haven't you heard? This is dumb-ass class. That's what they think and I let them."

"Why?"

"It's good to keep the powers that be in the dark. When

you're planning a revolution, it's best to keep your head down till it's time to strike. Then you take them all at the same time. The element of surprise. That's the way Custer got done in."

"Who's Custer?"

"That's why you need to be in here. We're learning more than how to lay down rhymes."

The kid looks at the others at the computers and nods his head and says, "Yeah, maybe."

That's the way I do. I pick up the strays. No one wants them, no one except me. Where I grew up, on the dirty-dirty south side, it's the strays that survive. A dog on the streets lives on his own, by his smarts, his willingness to do what he needs to do to live another day. You can learn a lot from watching them. Mexicans are strays. I'm a stray. These kids are strays. Together, we'll show the dogcatchers and tear down the pound.

§ § §

The truth is, I don't like the other teachers. They're sell-outs and squares. I like hanging with my students. We kick it in the classroom till the janitors make us leave. I give the boys, Juan (who goes by Banger), Oscar, Tito, and Tarasco rides home. They all live in Duros. All of them except Tarasco are gangsters. I don't know if they're serious bangers or not. So far, I haven't heard about any major beefs between any of the groups. But there's a lot of violence, mostly drugs. Thermal and Coachella are central for drug running. They use the kids to move the stuff in the desert cities and to move *coca* and *chiva* up to L.A.

For a couple of days, Banger doesn't come in after school and I ask his homies where he's at. "He's got home problems," says Oscar.

"What kind of home problems?"

"His pops is after his ass for something. He's just out of the joint, I think. He's been following him around, bugging him. I think he wants money or something. He got rolled on a drug beef and was locked up a long time. I don't know, but Banger's wigging. His moms is dead and the *vato* don't want nothing to do with his pops."

"That's bad news," I say. "What happened to his mom?"

"She got killed by a *pinche indio* coming out of a casino. He was drunk as a motherfucker. Banger's all fucked up," says Oscar.

"Fucked up how?"

"That fool's serious crazy. But he's *firme*. He don't back down and he's always got your back."

When Banger comes back, I talk to him. "You know I want you in this class. We need you in this class. But you got to come to school or they're going to tie my hands. You keep missing, and they'll expel you. It matters to me, but it won't to them." He nods, but he's got real problems and being expelled doesn't make the list. That's the big challenge with trying to work with these kids. School and all the rah-rah stuff isn't even on the radar for them. They have problems most people can't imagine. So you have to sell it. You have to keep at them, give them a reason to believe that what you're pushing is relevant to how they live.

You are born white. Blind luck. You are born in the United States. Blind luck. You are born into a cushy middle-class home. Blind luck. You are born into a family that gives a damn. Blind luck. But you'd never know it by watching the legals. They're the chosen ones, see? They worship a God who cares about them. He's going to get them into Heaven, the ultimate hook-up. Everyone else can suck it because if you're brown, black, poor, illegal, ignorant, homeless, befucked, that is your doing. I can't swallow it down anymore. My gut burns with it. The rich and the good citizens alike, going about their lives oblivious to the suffering, to the poverty, feeling entitled to their luck. Blind luck.

I drive by the country clubs, the wide avenues crowded with Mercedes, Jaguars, BMWs, and Hummers, and I imagine throwing gasoline on the whole thing, striking a match, and watching it all burn down. That's what these kids want too. The bangers, the *cholos*, the *pintos*, and *rancheros*; the dispossessed want to strike that match if only they had it. And everyday I go into that classroom and tell them, preach to them, that they do have something. But they need to focus the flame otherwise they're the ones who'll get burned. They have *ganas*, the will to survive, I tell them. But a lot of the time, in fact, on most days, I feel like it's a load of bullshit.

So I smoke *yesca* every chance I get. I fill the bowl when I get up and smoke it down. When I get home, I load another and another and I smoke them down. And the fire inside gets turned down just a notch, just enough so that

I can think clearly instead of giving into the anger. And then there's strippers. There's the calming effect of that thing they shake in your face. I'll blow through my meager paycheck on lap dances and weed. If you want to point your self-righteous finger, go ahead. You do it for a month. You come here with your pretensions, your ideals, your notions about how things work and how and who can be saved. You bet your ass, you'll be looking for the proverbial gun, finger at the trigger, ready to go off on someone, anyone, that's responsible for the misery.

It's like the girl I followed up here, Gloria. She came up with the best of intentions, but the scene chewed her up. I saw it grind her down. All the tears, her frustration when kids she was working with and had grown attached to, disappeared. No explanation, no warning, no forwarding address. Just gone. Around here, that's the rule. You work with a kid, get to know them, spend months reaching them, and then poof, like a cruel magic trick. The breaking point came when this poor girl she'd taken under her wing, only 15, pregnant, four sisters, all younger, all probably headed in the same direction, got yanked out of school and sent back to Mexico by her father. Gloria cried for a week. She thought that she could convince her parents to let the girl give the baby up. But they had other plans. That's the way it is here. Even thick skin wears thin.

There's not much to do when you're in the system because the system sets all the boundaries, all the parameters. It has the power to silence you, to keep you in line. And when the problems start, when you pull your head out of your *culo* long enough to see that even your little bit role is ultimately part of the corrupt and amoral and uninterested system at large, you either quit, grow cynical, or begin to take out the slow burn on the victims, the kids and their hapless parents. I know teachers who hate their students. It's easier to blame the kids for their poverty and ignorance, for the ways they slouch around, for the ways they don't look at you in the eye because they're afraid or because their clothes are shabby. You can't eradicate the system, the callousness of it all, so your eye turns towards the most vulnerable, because they can be eradicated. And don't they deserve it anyway? And your inward eye changes slowly, gradually so that you don't see them as kids anymore. You see *Them*, a mass that amounts to an insurmountable problem that mocks your efforts and your anger gets redirected. That's what's happened to so many of my so-called colleagues. Maybe Gloria was right to leave before it happened to her.

So I smoke weed. It gives me just enough separation to let me see that lots of us are just trying to get by, using what we've been taught, even if it's all wrong, to hang on a little longer.

§ § §

Tarasco hasn't been in class for three days, so I pay a visit to Duros. I find his mother's shack, park my car out in front and knock on the door. A dog, skinny and scared, crawls under the rickety porch afraid that I'm there to do him some harm. Tarasco opens the door, peeking out, scared like the dog that I'm there to do something to him.

"What's up, homie?" I ask him.

He shrugs, the door opens only a crack. "Nothing."

"You don't like school anymore? I smell bad or something?" He doesn't say anything, his expression staying the same. But he opens the door a little wider. "You need to come back. I need you in the classroom to teach the other knuckleheads who don't get it."

"Yeah," is all he says. I can see that he's taken a beating. His face has got some scratches on it, and his lip is swollen.

"What happened to your face?" I ask him. He doesn't say anything. "Who beat you up? You piss off a girl?" But I know it was his mom. She's a drunk. She gets wasted, gets mean about having to stoop over the strawberries all day long, about not having food or anything nice. No prospects, just a mule in the sun. And she gets home, drinks, and then strikes at what's closest at hand. It's an old story, old for everyone but the ones stuck in it.

"Look," I tell him, "I want you back in the classroom, *vato*. If I gotta come pick you up, I will. But I don't want you slipping up. You understand?"

He nods.

"I mean it. You need me here to get you in the morning?" He shakes his head. "Okay then, little bro, I'm going to see you tomorrow, right?"

"Okay," he nods his head. I walk back to the car and drive off in a cloud of dust hoping the kid will be at school the next day.

One of the locals who Principal Joe introduced me to is an old *veterano* named Leo who runs the community center in the Coachella Valley. From what I can see, the guy is *firme*. He gets things done. He invited me to a meeting of the minds, a pow-wow of the folks out here who get paid to give a damn and those who do it because they want to see things change around here. There's about fifty organizations trying to compete with each other for dough. All of them seem to have good intentions, all of them with pet projects dealing with things like better dental care, depression awareness, recreational park lights, bike trails, breast cancer awareness, diabetes screening, alcoholism, and a list of other initiatives. Then there's the sociologists and social workers, grad students, and other assorted observers who want to write about the rampant poverty and social dysfunction. They sit there drinking bottled water, in bad sports jackets and cheap shoes, passing pamphlets out to each other. It doesn't seem like these characters ever get anything done. But at least I meet people and meeting people is good. It's useful because if you've got a mission, you need resources and you never know who is going to come through. The bottom line is keep your eyes and ears open, make friends where you can, allies who will let you know things. Information can be better than money if you know how to use it.

Leo is smart that way. He doesn't fall for the bureaucratic game. He knows it can only take you so far. After the meeting, me, him, his son Henry, who is a wounded vet, and an older guy who drives, go to eat. Leo's wolfing a *lengua taco*, talking with his mouth full, taking big gulps of beer in between bites and telling me how things work here.

"I've been here more than forty years. And I can tell

you that there's always chicken suckers out to get what they can get, whether it's a rinky-dink title or some *feria* to throw around town. Not everybody who's supposed to be here for *la raza* is here for *la raza*. I can get things done here without all the committee horseshit. You have to play the game to a certain extent. But when you want results, it's better to get it done yourself. You start taking opinion polls around here, and you'll sit around with your thumb up your *culo* till the stink won't never go away."

I nod. I can learn things from Leo, who's been around the block a time or twenty. He's a good guy. His driver is an ex-con who Leo is helping out. He's a quiet guy. He eats his tacos and listens but doesn't say much. His name is Juan and he drives the *migros* to the showers during the day. He looks like someone who might know where to score weed. I try and sound him out on it while Leo is in the can, but he acts like he doesn't know what I'm talking about. Probably has two strikes on him. Henry, Leo's son, is talking about computers. "Learned it in the service." Leo's asked me if I can use Henry as a volunteer at the school. I said sure. I can always use the help. "I told the kids you're going to be helping out," I tell him. "I'm glad you've got the time."

"Got nothing but time," he says. Leo comes back. He walks like his mama pushed him out onto horseback at birth. Dude's bowlegged.

"So what are you doing here?" he says getting to the bottom line.

"Stirring up trouble, I guess."

"Is that all? Won't take you too much time to do that around here. Your average *pendejo* finds it in no time flat."

"I want to stir up trouble for the *pinche gabachos* trying to keep everything under wraps around here," I say. "But mostly, I want to help my kids. As best as I can tell, doing one means doing the other." Leo nods as he works on a fresh beer.

"There's going to be a march," he says. "It would be good for your kids to turn out. Maybe they can film some of it for the news."

"That'd be good," I say. "But we're trying to do something bigger. They're making a movie to show everybody how things here work. The plan is for them to tell their own stories and put them right on the Internet and make somebody pay attention. It's going to get so that they can't ignore us," I say. "We've got some things in the works. We're going to take on the Indian tribes, make them stop taking money from the builders to burn all that toxic waste in Duros."

"That's sure to piss a lot of people off," Leo says. "That's big money for everyone involved."

"I guess they're not happy enough with the casinos, huh?"

"When have you ever heard anybody being happy enough? This is America, son."

"How much money are we talking about?"

"Around 50k a month, at least," Leo says.

"That much?"

"We're talking dangerous chemicals, carcinogens, pesticides, benzene and PCB's and asbestos. Shit they don't even test out on lab rats," Leo says.

Henry says, "That's the way we do out in Iraq. We don't give a damn about what or who we burn there."

"I got a little girl in my class. Her name is María and she's dying from leukemia," I tell them. "Lot's of other kids have asthma and who knows what else. Who's going to do something about it?"

"Maybe you," Leo says. "The *LA Times* sent some *gabacho* reporter here a couple of years ago. Nothing but shrugs. The EPA ordered the place shut down back in the 80s. No one enforced it. The burning goes on."

"We should march on that," I say.

"Bring them to ours," Leo says. "I'll lend you the van to transport, if you think it'll help."

"Can you help drive?" I ask Juan.

"I don't know," he says. "My kid lives in Duros. He doesn't need any more trouble in his life. What you're talking about just brings more problems."

"Your kid go to school at Mirage?"

"Yeah. His name is Juan."

"Juan what?"

"Juan Acuña."

"He's in my class. I just signed him up," I tell him. His father nods as he blows smoke. He's been chain smoking since we got here. "They call him 'Banger,' right?"

Juan, Sr. looks at me and says, "I didn't know that." He takes a final swig of his beer, nods at Leo and me both, and walks off towards the van to smoke another cigarette.

So the march is set, and Principal Joe is going to let me use the cameras. He's even giving permission for the kids to leave school early to attend. "I remember the old days," he says. "Keep a tight watch on things. Things can get tricky fast. It's got to be peaceful and dignified. It isn't going to do any good if you give the community the proof they need to keep treating these kids like subhumans." He runs his fingers through his Pancho Villa mustache. "There's always a bunch of bastards out there trying to bring the old days back. So do what you can," he says. "But do it right."

§ § §

Tarasco shows me his first movie. It's only two and a half minutes long. It's taken as the sun sets, the mountains that look brown and bare in the searing daylight, coming alive in colors only the desert brings together. The camera pans slowly, Los Duros' harshness made small by the rocky hands that beckon from far into the horizon. It's as if they are telling the viewer that the ugliness will pass. It's not permanent. Greed and indifference have only a limited reach. The earth abides in spite of the cruelty perpetrated on these people. I don't tell him this shit, of course. I tell him that it's good, that he has an eye, that he has talent. Tarasco nods, even managing a short, small smile. I ask him if he wants to get something to eat after school. He says, "Okay," about as much as he ever says.

We drive to a taco joint on the outskirts of Thermal. It's a hole, but the *barbacoa* is good. When it's just us two, the kid opens up. In school, he's so quiet, you'd think he was a cat burglar. He does everything not to be noticed, but because he's so big and tall, with big, dark Asiatic brown eyes, he's become a kind of mascot for the other kids. They don't taunt him or give him much crap, but they say to him,

"Tarasco, don't be sneaking up on me like that!" The girls giggle around him and this makes him nervous, his eyes never making contact as he wheels around and makes for the farthest side of the room.

"Do you like it here?" I ask him as we eat.

"No," he says. I wait for something else, but he stops.

"Why not, aside from Duros?"

"I want to go back home. But my mom says we have to stay."

"You're almost old enough to roll out on your own. Why don't you?"

He thinks about it. "Because she'll die if I leave."

I drop it there because it's probably true. It's sad that his mother's an alky, that she slaps him around. But you only have one mother, I guess. Mine was a good woman. Did everything she could with me and my brothers. We didn't make it easy on her after my father died. But she did what she could to keep us off the streets, including beating our asses when it came down to it. We still ran the streets, but at least we were afraid of her. She sends me care packages. Junk she's bought at the *pulga* in San Antonio, mostly pirated Spurs T-shirts that shrink up around my fat belly. She sends me Mexican candy, last week, a Virgin Mary icon that lights up rave-style and that's right now hanging around my thick, brown neck. La Virgen might not be able to protect me, but at least my ass won't get run down by a car at night with her red light eyes flashing like a strobe light.

"Well, don't be taking off just yet," I say to Tarasco as we finish up. "I want to talk to you about your movie. That was good. Real good. I gotta keep telling you that. That thing moved me and I'm hard to move. I want you to make another one. I want you to find something in Los Duros that you'd never expect to see, something that if you didn't live there, that if you were some scared-ass Palm Springs type, you'd never come across. I want to make it part of this documentary we're putting together to shut down the dump."

Tarasco shows as much excitement as he ever does, a slight upturn of his lips, a light in his eyes that he can't hide. I drop him off and tell him to get after it. The sun is going down and Los Duros is growing dark. Only a couple of trailers have lights, those that can afford a personal generator. The streets are shadows and all of the children are inside. It's a sad place covered in silence and gloom.

§ § §

The kids are psyched. They've each contributed something to the documentary. The deepest is an interview with María, her pale face skinny from the leukemia, patches of acne showing up bright red in contrast to her white skin. She's got purple bruises along her arms and legs. She's dying. Her friend asks her if she's afraid of what will happen to her. "I'm afraid for my sister, afraid that she'll get it too," she says.

The interviewer asks, "Do you think you got sick from the chemicals, from the pollution?"

María nods, her little sister in the background, curious and shy about the camera, her fingers in her mouth as she looks on. "I don't like to think about what will happen when I'm gone."

"What do you think will happen?"

"It'll go on just like always."

You'd have to be a monster for that not to hit you in the balls. But believe me, there's a lot of them out there. I can barely take watching the news or reading the newspapers. Every day some new bastard is raving about illegal aliens, about the *Reconquista*, about the illegals who are no better than cockroaches. But what if they had to face María? What if they had to look into her yellowed eyes, see her parched lips, her eyes sinking into her beautiful face? Would she be alien to them? Wouldn't they recognize something in her dying beauty? Their own children?

I work hard to remind myself and the kids that there is still some power in action, still some power in truth. "We've been here a long time," I can hear Leo telling me, "and we'll outlast them because suffering makes us strong. It always has. It always will." But when I look at María, when I look at these kids with their torn shoes and their dingy clothes, Leo's words seem like nothing but wishful thinking. Canned words saved up for another useless rally.

Some stuff goes down at the march. A couple of scuffles, mostly some of the kids shouting at a group of counter-protesters holding up American flags and posters that say, "This is Our Country," and "Go Home!" Our kids are wearing Mexican flag T-shirts or holding up posters of Zapata, Pancho Villa, and *Comandante Z.* They want to identify with people who stood up for the poor and the despised.

The kids know that they're seen as human garbage, like the sludge that's left after the fire in Duros. It's not just *gabachos* who tell them this. It's the cops, the media, the politicians, the shit parts of town they have to live in, the blood and sweat that's never admired or acknowledged, let alone rewarded. I was talking to another teacher in the lunchroom about four of my kids who were interested in going to college. She acted surprised that they even knew what college was. After about a couple of beats, she says, "Well, be careful, because illegals aren't allowed to go to college in this country. You have to be realistic."

So reality is no more than picking grapes, strawberries, and lettuce, tarring roofs, taking care of rich people's kids. Mow the lawns, spread manure, work in the coal mines and the slaughterhouses. Just don't get any smart ideas about something bigger or better.

"There's places, there's states," I told her. "I got connections. Not every state is as jacked up as California." She didn't say anything, but I had her number.

I'm not sure how much good it will do, but at least the march feels good. Even the scuffles feel good. Just showing up and yelling back, telling the citizens of the jewel cities and their reporters that we are here and that they're not just going to drag our asses back to Mexico like they did during Operation Wetback in the 50s. It's a beautiful sight, the *mojados* and *rancheros* and *cholos* marching side by side, saying, "You won't snatch me off the street without a fight, without us making noise!" We film it all. The hundreds of brown kids and their parents, sweating in the heat, proud of their heritage, letting each other know that they have a voice. Every day, they are treated as if they are invisible. In fact, they are trained to prefer invisibility. One of my students, Leticia, takes the bullhorn, a big gray one that looks like it might've seen action during the strikes forty years ago, and says, "Lay low, don't talk so loud, don't look anyone in the eye, don't speak up, don't give your opinion, shut up and work hard, don't complain, don't call attention to yourself. It's all we hear. That's what they want, but not today." And the crowd reacts with cheers. When the trouble starts, I make sure to keep my kids clear of it. We have different tactics.

After, I meet with a group of kids who want to put their energy into a specific issue. "How about we demand that the *indios* and the city shut down the dump?" We decide we'll finish the documentary, post it on the web, and send it to all the newspapers, to the TV stations, to whoever will care. We'll let them know what's going on down here. They're hyped. They talk about making T-shirts with their new slogan, "Stop the Burning!" Tarasco is hiding behind a computer, but he's listening. He wants to be part of it. After the other kids split, I ask him, "So you down with editing our Barriomentary?"

"Me?" he asks.

"Yeah, you. You're the best with these programs. You already know as much as I do about the film program, maybe more. Hell, you spend all day on it." He thinks a bit, all the while looking at the screen.

"I could try," he says.

"Do more than try, Tarasco. I want some Academy Award type shit. We gotta make the soft-hearted cry and the hardhearted feel shame."

"I don't think it'll work," he says.

"Why not?"

"No one feels shame unless they get caught at something."

"We are catching them at something. They're poisoning people, they're poisoning the earth. It don't get more shameful than that." He nods, but he's not convinced.

The Spotlight Casino is owned by the same tribe that owns the land where Duros sits. I go there for drinks. I know it's ironic, but it's the only place in this desert unless you head to one of the jewels with their upscale bullshit. I throw away a couple of twenties at the slots, smoke cigarettes, and hang out with the one buddy I've made here besides the kids. He's kind of a *flecha*, a straight arrow. Roberto won't smoke weed with me, but he'll drink a little and even sneak a cig when his wife isn't around. He's a science teacher at the school and he's going to give the documentary some authority by talking about what the toxins do to the people in Duros.

"It's everybody in this region that suffers the consequences of this poison," he says. "It's not just Los Duros. The kids are only the canaries in the coalmine."

"Well this time the canaries aren't just going to die quiet," I say. "We're going to squawk till somebody wakes up." Roberto smiles at this, but then he goes serious on me.

"You thought about what's going to happen if people really start paying attention?"

"Hell yes," I say. "That's the point, Beto. We want mofos

to pay attention. We want to shove the pollution down their throats so they'll shut it down."

"No," he says. "I mean the people who make money off this. You're messing with someone's money. They won't like it. They may not kill you, but they can make life real tough for you. Maybe get you fired or arrested or whatever."

"I got a .38 in my glove compartment," I say. "Anyone comes at me gets a cap blasted in their ass."

"C'mon," he says. "I'm not joking. You haven't been here long enough to see how they operate. They control everything here. The casinos, the cops, the city council. They own the businesses, pay the taxes, run the elections."

"Who? The *indios*?"

"Not really. They've got some say because they've got lots of new money. But I'm talking about those who make money off the *indios*, the casinos, the burning, the pesticides. The Them, Guillermo. That's who I'm talking about. You think it's black and white, but it's really just white and white."

"Yeah, well they better worry about us, because we're not screwing around."

"I hope you're not. This is serious business. I'm from here. You're not. I hope it's not some half-assed reliving of the *Movimiento*. People got their heads busted back then. They lost a lot. I know. My father lost his house and his health in the *huelgas*. A lot of people lost everything for the movement. And for what? Not all that much has changed."

"Ah, man, don't go soft on me," I say.

"I'm not. I'm just telling you that so far you've been dealing with kids, having them film things for class. It's been fun and games. But if you start shining a light into this corner, you're going to find out that these people know how to protect their assets, whether those assets are toxic waste dumps, cheap labor, power, or privilege. It isn't any accident that they live up in the hills and we live in the valleys. Look around."

"I know," I say. "I've been doing nothing but looking. It's time to do something. I have never run from throwing *chingazos* and I sure as hell ain't going to start now. These bastards have a fight coming to them."

"Nah," Roberto says. "You're not getting it. These kids and their people have to live here if and when they chase you off. I know the solidarity vision is real for you, but you're not one of them. You can't be. You're not a friend, you're not a *migro*, you don't live in Duros. You have to think about that."

"You're wrong," I tell him. "This place is my home now."

§ § §

María died this morning.

At a county hospital, tubes running in and out of her arms, her face drawn and pale, her life force drained like her shriveled iv. Her grandmother sat stoically, grief evident only in her swollen eyes. This old woman, heavy with the load of tragedies she'd witnessed in her life, the shit poverty of Los Duros, the back-shattering work in the fields, had seen it all, at least until her 14-year old granddaughter died slow in front of her.

I walked into the hospital room and gave her my condolences. She looked at me, maybe not recognizing. She didn't say much, just gave me her dark brown calloused hand as she made a quiet nod. It was María's little sister that showed grief for all of us. She was like a small wounded animal, no words to articulate her loss and pain, just a low moaning that would from time to time slide up into a high-pitched wail. Her mom tried to comfort her, but she didn't want to be comforted. She was too young to know what death was, but she knew she wasn't getting her big sister back.

"Where are they going to take her?" I asked an uncle who waited outside in the hall with some other relatives.

"There's a place," he said.

The funeral was small, a few dozen people, half of them kids from the school who'd known her, mostly my kids. Tarasco came with me. He was as stone-faced as the grandmother, his eyes staring straight ahead as the Mass played out. When it came time to view the body for the last time, he hung back until the other kids and relatives had moved outside into cars for the burial. He went up alone, stood next to María, looked down at her. It was then that I realized that he'd felt something for her. Maybe he'd seen her every day in Duros, maybe he'd watched her walk down the dirt streets with her little sister in tow carrying laundry. Maybe he'd craved for her warm, brown skin, her thick, straight black hair that she parted in the middle and tied behind her in a loose ponytail. When we'd filmed the interview with her, one of her final acts before she got really bad, I remember that he'd spent a lot of time looking at her, even smiling, something Tarasco didn't do all that much.

I walked up to him, his hulking body, his large pumpkin head bowed, and put my arm around him. He didn't jump or move. He let me lay my arm across his shoulders.

"She was a good girl," I said for both of us. The boy nodded without saying anything. "We'll make her death mean something," I said, but it was more for myself because I wanted to believe that it was possible. The funeral workers who'd been waiting for everyone to leave so that they could screw on the top of the casket, came forward. As they approached, Tarasco put something in with María.

We walked outside and got into my truck. "What was that you put in there?" I asked him as we drove towards the cemetery. But he wouldn't tell me. It was a secret, his and María's secret and it made me feel low somehow, like nothing could come from this that would be worth a good goddamn for any of these kids.

§ § §

But something does come of it. Maybe María's spirit made it so that someone sees the documentary on the website the kids have set up. Some producer from the local PBS station in Palm Springs. He wants to air it. "We think that it's important from a human rights perspective," he said. "Environmentally, this is a disaster for this entire area. People should know what's going on right under their noses." He wanted to re-cut the movie, wanted his pro editors to spend a little time polishing it. But I told him no. This is a film by *cholitos, rancheros*, and *mojados*. It airs as is, although I offered to have the kids work on it some more. There's a new energy, a sense of mission, the idea that we're doing this for María and her sister, for all the Marías and asthmatic kids in Los Duros. It cuts through the sadness, gives the kids hope that someone gives a damn, that they can make a difference.

It's a short video. Only twelve minutes. A long focus shot of the Salton Sea with Roberto the science teacher giving the facts of the rampant pollution, the dumping, the pesticides, the chemicals that end up in the water, the fish kills, the nausea that comes with toxic levels like this. And then a fade to black with the entrance to Los Duros appearing after a moment of darkness. Then the face of María, weak and dying, but more alive than anything else in the film. I don't want to romanticize it. You should see it. It breaks your heart to see her smile and talk about what she wants to do with her life. As the camera pulls back a little, we see her little sister and she tells in her little kid way, how she's not allowed to play outside because the air makes her cough. And then another fade out that connects to the final scene where we see the black smoke of the burning dump, the poisoned air drifting back towards the shacks and hovels of Los Duros. An off camera voice says,

"This is our home, our *barrio*, our *colonia*. Our brothers and sisters live here, our *abuelos* die here. We want justice for the environment, for Los Duros, for our families, for our planet." Then a dedication with María's picture and her birth and death dates.

It is stark and raw and moving, an indictment of the indifference to mute suffering. And after the show airs, just three weeks after María dies, the hell I was expecting, wanting, breaks loose. The newspapers are suddenly on this like the black flies on the rotting fish of the Salton Sea. College students call and email asking how they can support the cause. The Sierra Club and other environmental groups want to get in on the action. We set up plans for a big march, a march from the Salton Sea to the Los Duros dump. But the Indians aren't having it, the mayor's not having it, the city council, and the Chamber of Commerce, the polluters, the builders, the moneyed fuckers who run the desert, begin to make noise. No permit. And the students begin to get angrier and angrier. I see it in Tarasco's face. I see it in the eyes of the bangers like Juan and his crew.

Henry, Leo's son, who's now helping out a couple of times a week says, "Something is going to give." He seems like someone who would know.

§ § §

Leo called me with the news. The EPA, the city council, the chamber of commerce, Bureau of Indian Affairs, and "concerned citizens," have spoken up demanding that the burning be stopped. The catch is that they've also called for shutting down Duros. The "illegal aliens" living there have to leave or be rounded up and shipped back to where they came from. Someone has to pay.

That's the deal. Close the gates, push them all out like toy balloons to drift off somewhere else. Those will be the lucky ones. Others will get caught up in ICE net. Nothing too serious, just enough aliens to satisfy the Palm Springs crowd.

"So that's it?" I say. "That's the solution?"

"That's the usual solution," Leo says. "Hell, I didn't see it coming either, but I've been around here long enough that I should've known better. They're even leaning on me. The mayor's office let me know, 'Don't cause any trouble on this, Los Duros has got to go.' If I make noise, they cut off funding for the showers, the clinic, and the center, all of it. They don't want any more bad press."

"What are you going to do?"

"Not much to do, Guillermo. We can protest. It won't do much good. It's all set now. The EPA will send some of their boys out to the site to make sure it's cleaned up some. The Indians will have to foot the bill, maybe pay a fine. ICE will come in and sweep Los Duros, although most of the people will leave on their own. There's lots of *colonias* in these parts for them to crowd into. There's still crops to be picked, lawns to be mowed, houses to be built."

"I thought we were going to make things better," I say like a dumbass.

"C'mon, son," Leo says, "'better' is relative. You gave these kids something important to do. They did it. Now they'll have to learn that in this world doing the right thing has a price." But through the tough words, Leo can't hide that he's been punched in the gut.

I get to school on Monday worried about telling the kids what to expect. But the network is quick and bad news moves through the community fast. I'm surprised because they don't seem very worried. Most of them gaze back at me matter of fact, like I've told them to expect hot weather. Banger says, "What did you expect, Teach? They're always going to push us around. At least this time, we made some noise about it."

The kids are proud, proud that they've been the cause of something. I try to apologize to them, but they're in no mood to hear it. It makes it worse. But Principal Joe and some of the teachers aren't letting me off the hook. They're grumbling, giving me sideways looks, blaming me and my kids for bringing trouble.

Principal Joe comes into my classroom at the end of the day. He walks in, mustache drooping, his small eyes fixed on me.

"I'm not here to bullshit," he says. "The school board's let me know that I shouldn't have approved the use of school equipment for political purposes. There's been a lot of heat these last couple of years. The politicians and the xenophobes are getting after it, and this attention is going to make it worse for the kids."

"How can it get worse for us?" I say.

"Look," he says, "I told you I'm not here to bullshit. I've been fighting the good fight since before you were born, and I know these people, the brown ones and the white ones. You do what you can. You look for opportunities. You make gradual progress, slow and steady. But you don't do it by getting in people's faces. So no more cameras or using the computers for your political films. Anything that gets done in here using our equipment, any assignments you give, has got to be cleared by me. You got it, Guillermo?"

I don't say anything for a second. He stands there, looking at me. Finally I say, "Whatever you say, Principal Joe."

"You need to get it straight. You're not living in their shoes. Being a teacher, a mentor, means knowing that there's a difference between these kids and you. You're not here to be a friend or a political leader. You're here to instruct. Computers, remember?"

"Like I said, whatever you say." I figure, fuck him and his school board. What I'm going to do, what we're going to do, we're going to do, and nobody's going to stop us.

As for Los Duros, no one is prepared for anything. The ones that can will leave for other towns farther north, Fresno, Sacramento, Delano. A few will find another *colonia* to move to. There's plenty. Some who have relatives in the area, will move with them till they can find something else. The ones who have no choice will stick around Los Duros till ICE starts rounding people up, till the sheriff comes out with his deputies and starts throwing people out of their shacks and trailers. The parking lot at Lenchos Grocery will get a lot more crowded. Life will get tougher. But that's what *They* want. This is an object lesson for all the illegals who thought they could speak out about things and get away with it. It looks like *They* did the real teaching.

My kids want to march again. Oscar says, "We don't want to lay down without a fight." He's got about ten kids with him, including Tarasco and Banger, who stand at the back of the group. Tarasco's head sticks out above all the others.

"That's what you want?" I ask them. "That's just going to piss off these people even more. They might want to bust heads if you kids keep on pointing out how badly you're getting screwed."

Banger says, "We ain't going out like that."

"Good," I say. I feel like somebody ought to pay for this shit too. For María and her little sister and all the little sisters out there that are going to wind up in the street, swept up like pieces of trash in the wind. "But this has got to be peaceful," I say. "I know we want to break out and burn shit down, but that won't get us anywhere. We've got to let them know we mean business. But business is making people aware of what's happening around here. Otherwise, these people will use it as an excuse to do their worst."

"Fuck 'em, Teach," Banger says.

I want to say, "Yeah, fuck those *gringo* motherfuckers." But I don't want anyone getting thrown in jail or worse. So instead I say, "Yeah, fuck 'em, but let's do it so that they look bad, so that we expose them. We'll film the whole thing again, just like Los Duros, and we'll put it on the Internet. We'll get the newspapers and news cameras back out here. You'll see. We'll wake them all up."

The kids take off, except for Tarasco and Banger. "You still living in Duros?" I ask Banger. He nods his head. "I met your old man when I was hanging out with Leo and Henry. You don't live with him?"

He shakes his head, "Nah, man, I live on my own. I take care of myself. I even wipe my own ass these days."

"That's good," I say. "I ain't here to wipe nobody's behind. But check yourself on any ideas about letting this shit break out into a street fight. That isn't going to get anyone anywhere."

But Banger's anger goes deeper than the Duros situation. A lot deeper. I don't know all of where it's coming from. I need to defuse it, at least focus it on something positive.

"Where do you want all this to go?" I ask him.

"Don't know," he says. "You're the Teach, right?"

The problem is that things are happening too fast, and I'm not sure myself. I only know I don't want to let these kids down. "We don't do anything till we think this through. We have to be smart. We have to get each other's backs. We're in this together, all of us."

They want to pull off a protest on Monday, a walkout, students from the middle school and the high school leaving their classrooms, shutting down the school. "Like the Brown Outs," one of the kids points out. They're looking for my permission.

"Lots of people went to jail for the Brown Outs," I warn them.

"You scared, Teach?" Banger asks.

"You're a dumbass if you're not scared of jail. I want you all to know that there'll be some blowback, things you don't expect. No one thinks Mexicans should say shit about shit, and especially young ones like you. There'll be consequences. We have to do this thing right."

"What they going to do?" Banger says. "Throw us out of Duros twice?" Some of the kids laugh.

"That's what I wanted to hear," I say. "But we have to keep our cool. Remember what our mission is. Let them know we're here, let them know we're not going to be silent."

I get a hold of some of the newspapers, a couple of radio stations, even a couple of Chicanos I know working in TV in L.A. and Riverside. We put the word out: fliers, webpage, Mexican radio.

Principal Joe comes after me first. "We can't have these kids walk out," he says.

"I don't control what these kids do," I tell him.

"Cut the shit," he says. "If these kids get hurt or cause trouble, it's going to be on me and it's going to be on you."

"Like I told you, Joe, I don't control them. And I can't tell them to hold their tongues and play nice when these bastards are looking to fuck them some more. I won't do that."

"If this goes down, you're going to get fired," he says. "I don't want to do that. You're a good teacher and you're making a difference. Think about that. Do you think you'll be more useful leading some kind of riot? Nothing's going to come of it. This isn't the 60s. Even the 60s weren't the 60s. We make incremental progress. We do it by working the system. If you want to make change, you've got to be part of that. When are you going to learn?"

"I'm not part of all that," I say.

"Yes you are, Guillermo. So am I, so's this school. You think we'd have had something like this forty years ago?"

"A building isn't progress," I say.

"You're like a brick wall, huh?" He shakes his head looking me straight in the eye like a disapproving father. "You weren't alive in the old days when they'd just as soon beat you to a pulp as listen to your demands for a school, for minimum wage or toilets and water in the fields. Believe it, we've made progress. What you're encouraging is going to set us back. It's going to hurt these kids and their parents."

"Don't seem like progress to me, Joe. Don't seem to me like that at all. This beautiful school isn't for them. They built this place for the white kids whose wealthy families are already building those big houses outside Thermal. They'll put another goddamn golf course here pretty soon. And they'll push these kids and their families out because there isn't any room for Mexicans when the owners come to town."

Principal Joe shakes his head and walks out of the room, stopping in the doorway. "You better think hard about what you're doing, son."

Banger's father comes in the middle of the night. He knocks on my trailer door, waking me up from my couch where I'm sleeping off a drunk. I haven't seen him since the lunch with Leo. I open the door and he's standing out there, his cowboy hat in hand. I can smell the nicotine rolling off him like he's been chain-smoking since first grade. He looks worried, shifting from foot to foot.

"You're my boy's teacher," he says.

I nod. "What's wrong?"

"I'm sorry to bother you, but something's happened and I need your help."

"What?" I ask him.

"Juan's gotten himself into trouble."

"What happened?

"He's been in some kind of fight. He got arrested. I'm not too sure what's happened, only that the fight involved some white kids. I don't know how serious it is, but they've got him. I was hoping you could go down to the station with me."

"You're his father, so they should release him to you," I say. I'm still groggy, my head feeling too big to get through the doorway.

"It's that I've been in trouble before. Just got out a while ago and I think you can help so that they'll release him. Otherwise, they'll keep him, me having done time."

We get into his pickup and drive to Rancho Mirage. It's not the ideal town for a Mexican to get arrested in. The station is a big place, an office with a load of desks, holding cells upstairs, and more than enough cops on duty to protect a small town. He's been arraigned in juvenile court, which is good for him because he's seventeen and they could've gone the other way. They're going to hold onto the other kid who turns out to be Oscar. He's 18, an adult—and he's illegal. They've called ICE and they'll be there tonight more than likely. I try talking the cop out of this, but it's too late. No way. Oscar's screwed. He threw *chingazos* with some rich white kids. I'll let his parents know if I can find them.

Banger skulks out, skinny-ass trying to look tough. His T-shirt is torn to shit, his eye puffed up and a long scrape that runs from his forehead to his chin. Looks like whatever he got into fought back. "What happened?" I say after we've crowded into the father's small truck. The kid is in the middle, one foot on my side, the other on his father's side. He doesn't say anything.

Finally, the father tells him, "You heard your teacher. What happened? What did you do?" Banger doesn't want to talk, especially to his father.

"Looks like whatever you did," I say, "is going to get you into some real trouble. Oscar is already neck deep in it. They're going to ship him back to the homeland, *vato*. He's on his way back south, one-way ticket. You're lucky they didn't deport you too. Hell, half the time, these fuckers don't even ask for ID. I told you not to slip up, homie. You couldn't wait, huh?"

"What's he talking about, Juan?" the father asks. He's getting angrier and angrier at his slouching son. Banger doesn't like being asked anything by his old man. I can feel his shoulders square up, his body stiffening at the questions. "Some people have to learn the hard way," the old man says angrily.

"You don't have shit to say to me," Banger says looking straight ahead.

"You shouldn't talk to your pops that way," I tell him. The boy doesn't respond. "Who'd you hit and why?" I ask him.

"Some white punks," he says. "Motherfuckers had it coming and I'd do it again if I ran into them right now. They're lucky me and Oscar didn't kill them." At that, Juan Sr. hits the breaks all of the sudden, almost losing control of the truck which fishtails into the oncoming lane before it finally comes to a stop in the sandbar next to the road.

Banger's father slams the wheel with both fists. "You don't know what the hell you're talking about," he yells. "What do you know about killing anyone? You know what it's like to take a life, huh, big shot?" He turns half around and grabs the kid by the neck with his left hand, and Banger grabs the man's thick wrist with both skinny hands trying to curse his father, but he can only croak out and it sounds more like he's crying.

"Hey, man, cool it! You gotta let him go, Juan. Let your kid go. You're going to make things worse," I say trying to go around the kid to pry the man's hand from his throat. Juan finally lets go and he pounds the steering wheel again hard enough that he's lucky if he hasn't broken his hand. The boy is rubbing his neck and I can see in the dark that his eyes have teared up, although it's probably from being choked. "Hey," I tell the father, "you can't be doing that. I know you're upset, but this is only going to make things worse. You alright?" I ask the kid.

He doesn't say anything. He keeps rubbing his throat in silence. "You guys have to settle this thing without getting physical. Let's go back to my trailer and we'll see if we can't get to the bottom of all this." The father pulls the truck back out on the road. We head for my place.

When we get there, neither of them wants to talk, like neither has a thing to say, two strangers that look alike, mirrors, one showing the other a younger or older version of himself. Even their body language is the same. They both sit up straight, rigid, both looking at the wall in front of them like angry brothers. "Look, I don't know about your family business," I say finally. "I don't want to know. It isn't any of my business. All I'm about here is making sure nobody kills anyone. Whatever beef you have with each other, that's got to be something you can come to terms with. Life doesn't go on forever. I know, I lost my pops when I was a kid." I look at Banger. "I thought I had a lot to be pissed off at my pops before he died, but after, I couldn't remember a thing I'd been mad about. He was gone and that was that. Your old man's had some problems from what I've heard, but he's the only pops you're ever going to have and if your mom is gone, then maybe you ought to hear his side of things, whatever it may be."

The father turns to look at me while I address his kid and then he says, "He's got a right. I know that. He doesn't owe me anything."

That stumps me for a minute. I turn towards Banger. He's still sitting straight up, still eyeballing the wall of my trailer, where a yellowing poster of the San Antonio Conjunto Festival hangs. "Okay," I say to the father. "If you think he's got the right, then tell him."

The father sits there, his shoulders a little slumped now, his hand moving up to his mustache, stroking it as if he's contemplating a tough decision. He turns towards the boy, who still won't look at him, and he says, "You got every right to tell me to get lost. You've already done it and I don't hold it against you. I wouldn't be here unless you'd gotten in trouble. When they called me, I wanted to help."

"I don't need your help," Banger says. "I sure as hell didn't call you."

"I don't want you rotting in jail like I did," the father says. "That's why I came here, to see if I could," he stops talking. His son says nothing in response, his rejection hangs in the air like the nicotine stink.

"Where are you staying?" I ask the boy. "You still in Los

Duros? What you gonna do in the next couple of weeks when the sheriff comes to sweep everyone out?"

"I ain't going anywhere," Banger says. "Fuck them. They'll have to pull my ass out of my trailer. They're gonna have to drag a lot of Mexicans out of that motherfucker."

"I understand that," I say. "We're trying to march on that, but what if it doesn't work? More than likely, they're going to shut it down, and then what?"

"It won't work," the father says. "It just won't. There's no way to stop them when they want something. They want it, they take it and then worry about the consequences later, if ever. You don't spend ten years of your life in prison without learning that much."

"Why don't you give your pops a chance and try staying with him for a while? Things are going to be hot in Los Duros and the last thing you need is to get arrested again. The cops will be looking for trouble, any excuse to lock us up."

"I take care of myself," the kid says.

"Yeah, looks like you're doing a great job," I say.

"You don't know nothing about me, *ese*," Banger says. "You're my teacher, but that don't really mean shit, does it?"

"You're right about that," I say. "But I know when I see somebody getting too close to the edge. Maybe you ought to give your pops' wisdom at least one of your ears. You might have a legit beef with him for lots of things but you can't argue that the man doesn't have some hard won knowledge to drop on you."

Banger is too proud to give in even though I can sense

that there's a part of him that would like to. Finally, the father says, "Could he stay here with you for a while? Not too long."

"How much trouble would that cost me, homie?" I say looking at the kid hard. "I'm already enemy number one at the school. I don't need the cops coming out here and fucking with my shit on top of that."

The boy doesn't say anything, but his posture shifts a little. I can tell that he likes the idea, that he's listening, hoping we'll make the decision so that he doesn't have to give in.

"He'd watch himself. He doesn't want to cause you any trouble," the father says.

"That right?" I ask him. "You don't want to cause me any trouble?"

"I don't cause trouble for anyone but myself," he says finally.

"It may seem that way, but it isn't true. Look, you can crash here till you figure something out with your old man. But you gotta be useful. You know what I mean? We've got this march to try and make some noise about them shutting Los Duros down. That's some true trouble for a lot of families. You stay with me, you conserve your energy for taking this to the streets in a productive way. Understand?"

The boy nods. His father looks relieved. He wants to shake my hand like it's a business deal and he doesn't want me to change my mind. It's a sorry kind of sight, a father and son so distant from each other. It shouldn't be that way. But it is. I shake his hand.

§ § §

They fire me. They call it administrative leave without pay. They don't have to explain shit to me because I've never been fully accredited, never been in the Teacher's Union. I'm just a temp working on provisional credentials. Principal Joe comes to my classroom before school starts. He says, "I'm sorry but this one's come down from the school board. I warned you, Guillermo. They got wind of this march and they don't want any of our teachers involved with it. They don't want our students involved in it. They sure as hell don't want the school used as a rallying point. There's been enough trouble here these past couple of months without the added attention you seem hell-bent on bringing."

I look at him for a minute, trying to figure him out.

"You got something to say, you better say it now," Principal Joe says.

"I'm just wondering what happened to you, 'mano. I thought you marched with Cesar back in the day. I thought this was the place where it all started, the farmworkers, Chicanos, *indios*, all of us marching for our rights. What happened, huh?"

"I don't have time for this shit, son," he says. "You don't have a clue what it takes to get things done around here. You ride into town and think that you've got an angle on everything, that you're going to come in here and drive everyone into a frenzy by pointing out what everyone around here already knows. Everybody around here lives the racism and poverty. You aren't telling anyone anything new."

"I don't accept that."

Principal Joe gives me a half smile, angry and resigned at the same time. "Get your things out of here before school starts," he says. "I'm going to give the class over to Henry till we get a replacement. If we get a replacement. If you've got any problems with this decision, you take it up with the school board." He walks out the door and I see him talking to one of the security guards in the hallway.

"Sucks, dog," says the guard, a chubby Chicano I sometimes joke around with. "But you gotta go."

Tarasco shows up at my trailer that night. He's confused, so are all the kids. "Why weren't you at school?" he wants to know.

"It happens like that," I tell him. Banger is there too, eating a chili dog I made for dinner. "Hey, grab yourself a dog," I tell the big boy.

"You weren't there," he says again. "Why not?"

"I got my walking papers," I tell him.

"What does that mean?" he asks. He is standing next to the door, just inside the trailer.

"You're letting mosquitos in. Come in and close the door. Sit down, eat a chili dog and I'll explain it."

Banger looks up at us. "That's the way they do us up here," he says. "You two are new to this desert. You haven't seen the shit go down like I have. I've been here since I can remember and I ain't ever seen someone that they couldn't beat or chase the hell out of here if they want to."

"Are you leaving?" Tarasco asks. He is still next to the door, looking at me, his gaze unbroken by Banger's words.

"Not anytime soon," I say. "C'mon now, you're going to offend me if you don't come in and eat one of these goddamned chili dogs. Here, put some cheese on it." He comes in finally, taking a seat at the table next to Banger. Neither acknowledges the other. I put together a hot dog for the boy and bring it to the table. "Look, it's like this-- you make trouble for people, and they look for the quickest solution. Most of the time, firing someone or threatening them with cops or some other half-assed trick will work. But I'm not going anywhere till I see this through." Neither Banger nor Tarasco seems convinced by my words.

"What're you going to do?" Banger asks.

"We're going through with the march. We'll force it right down their throats. Start at the school and end up in Los Duros," I say.

"It's bad there," Tarasco says. "People are scared. My mom says we'll leave soon. Others have already packed up and gone. There was supposed to be a Mass there the other night, but the priest never came. An old man said a prayer, and not many people showed up."

"They're scared," Banger says. "Pussies."

"You're not scared?" I ask him.

"Of these *gabacho* motherfuckers? Nah, I ain't scared."

"That's a start," I say to both of them.

We stay in the kitchen a while longer talking about plans, about putting together a protest march that will make a statement. I realize that winning isn't a possibility, not really. We have to redefine winning because the game is always changing. They tell us one thing, promise us the just rewards of hard work, minding your own business, providing for your family, being a good citizen, all the while just waiting to ship you off, or cheat you, or shut you up and out. These boys, the *indio* and the *cholito*, they may be young, but they're not stupid. But what else is there to do? We have to try. We have to make some noise, even if all we can manage is a guttural howl.

But the march doesn't come off. Because sometime after midnight, after both Banger and Tarasco have left my trailer to pick up some clothes from Los Duros, there's a fire at the school. Someone has broken into my classroom—or what was my classroom—and struck a match. The entire building goes up in a four-alarmer. The next morning, the news reports that it was arson. Not long after, the cops are at my door with a shitload of questions.

3.

I'm like *kúmi-wátsï*, the fox. I know when to run, when to hide, when to lay low. You have to know how to listen. That's the most important thing when you don't have the words.

They don't know anything about us, about me. They blame me for being here, like I had anything to do with it. We're nothing but *chacas, pinche indios*. P'urhépecha is what we speak. To them it's gibberish, something to imitate because they don't understand it. And if they don't understand my tongue, what can they understand about me?

I'm a Tarascan from the highlands of Michoacán. My mom brought me here a year ago. I listen, I watch, I learn. I know more about them then they'll ever know about me. In the camp before, there were a few of us. We could stick together, talk, even laugh. But now in this school, the Tarascan kids are separated into different classes. It's better to keep quiet, stick to yourself, pretend you don't understand. They mostly leave you alone then. I sit with them as quiet as *kúmi-wátsï*. I stay alert. I'm always ready to run. It's the way you have to be when you don't belong anywhere.

My mom works in the fields all day. She drinks every night. She wants to die. She's been dying in pieces. Days like today, she dies just a little. She sits by the window after stooping in the sun. She drinks until the burning comes out. I don't blame her. I feel it too, the burning. I keep it inside. She lets it out through her mouth and hands. Tonight, she slaps me, the heat running out from her palms to my cheeks. I keep quiet. I'll know when to run. Until then, I hide in plain sight.

§ § §

Sometimes, I think I'll die before her.

§ § §

The Teacher sees me. I played the deaf-mute, the empty-head, but he found me and made me talk. At first I didn't want to. It's better to keep quiet, stay hid. But Teacher is a hunter and he found my hiding place. Now he's the hunted. I heard them talking.

"We know you had something to do with this or at least you know who did it," the policeman says.

"If I knew something, you think I'd still be here cooling it in this trailer? I'd be halfway to Mexico."

"This is serious. You got fired, right? That didn't sit too well. You're a troublemaker, stirring these kids up. And now your classroom is burned to shit. Hell, half the school is burned down. You really messed up, Peña."

"Look, I didn't burn shit. If you've got some kind of

proof, which you don't, then arrest me," Teacher tells them.

"Don't worry. We have plenty of reasons to arrest you. We know you've got a kid staying here, a minor, who happens to be a little thug. I'm sure if we toss this place, we'll find plenty of reasons to haul your ass in. So you'd better tell us what you know."

"Cops. Always with the angles, but you can't scare me because I haven't done anything and I don't know anything about any fire. Principal Joe canned me, but I wouldn't do any damage to the school. That's the only place a lot of those kids have. I wouldn't hurt them."

"That's sweet, real human of you. But we're on this thing. We've got experts on arson and we'll figure out who it was and if you're involved, you're going away for a long time."

The police left. They didn't see me because I had scooted under the trailer. I lay there for a while longer listening to Teacher pacing around. He talked to someone on the phone. He was mad, his voice as sharp as broken glass. After a while, I fell asleep. It was cool under there, a good hiding place.

I've got a lot of hiding places. Teacher's trailer, where he sometimes lets me stay when my mother's angry. There's a mountain that looks out at the Salton Sea. There's no trees there, but there's a place covered by an overhang of rock that I found when we first got here. I go there a lot. At the school, I hide behind silence. A few tried to flush me out, but they mostly gave up.

If you ask me what I miss most, it's that in the mountains where I come from, there isn't any reason to hide. Here, even the mountains hide from the roads and the men whose job it is to destroy anything silent. Where I'm from, the mountains and forests sit in plain sight. We live with them, not against them. My grandpa was a village elder, a fisherman who wove nets he used in Lake Pátzcuaro. He knew cures too. He knew about the ways animals behaved. He could make his way through the forest. He knew his way on the sea. He was quiet like me, big, with strong legs and arms that kept working hard until he died.

My mom didn't wait long. She put the few things that we could carry on our backs and we made our way here. She told me, "Look at this place and remember it. We won't be coming back." I tried to fix it all in my mind, but now I only remember it in bits and pieces, like a dream in another language. And even that, they want to take from me. The Mexican kids call me *chaca*, their word for shame. The teachers want to take my P'urhépecha. I won't let them. It's all I have left. That's why I hide, why I keep quiet, why I listen.

My mother never found my father. It's what kept her moving. Maybe he was never real. When she's drunk, she tells me he was a demon who raped her. "And then he flew away," she says in her slow drunk voice. "You have his ugly face." When she gets this bad, she loses control of her hands. They're rough, gnarled at the bones, the fingers swollen and crooked like the branches of a dead tree. They're strong, her hands, with sharp nails and callouses like sand that she rakes across my neck and face. Sometimes she does it while I'm asleep. The first time, I felt her over me as I lay on the mat on the floor. She stood above me for a few seconds, and

I could smell her drunk breath. When she struck, I hardly moved. It was my fault that I'd let her find me. I have to be more careful.

Teacher wouldn't let me hide. He found me outside the office at school when I threw my desk. It was stupid for me to lose it. That's how they find you. You let them hear your anger. I was angry because they want something from me, but they won't make it clear. So far all I can figure out is that they want for me to lie, to apologize for being mad, to pretend that I like it here. They want me to speak their language, give up my own, forget my grandfather, the mountains where I'm from. But if they can make you speak their way, they'll make you think their way.

"You can sit out here until you write your teacher an apology." I sat there for hours until Teacher noticed and talked to someone. They let him take me home. "You know what I'm saying?" he asked me on the ride. "You're a quiet *vato*," he said, "but I got a feeling you know a hell of a lot more than you let on. Why don't you come sit in my class tomorrow? We'll see what we can put you at." He was right.

When my mom isn't drinking, she tells me she loves me. She says it in our language, "*Pampzperaqua, vuache.*" "*Vuache*" means "my son." It means I belong to her. It means I have a past. When she's drunk, she calls me "*cunaricata*," a "bastard." This means I don't belong to her or my grandfather. I have no past. I have no present. This desert seems the right place for a *cunaricata*.

She wakes me in the morning before she goes to the fields in her torn clothes. She makes me go to school, even though some of the other Tarascan parents don't. She doesn't want me to die in Los Duros. The good that's left in her, that hasn't been dried out in the sun, is her hope for me. It's still there, this *mintzicani,* only there isn't much left. But Teacher has hope for me. He has hope for all of us. I don't think it'll come to anything.

Teacher is a hawk. He sees everything that happens in this place, in Los Duros, at the school, in Thermal, in the desert. You can't lie to him because he knows the lies. You can't hide from him because he'll find your hiding place. I've learned this from watching him.

§ § §

I want to say. But my tongue sticks to the back of my teeth, like a desert snail in its shell. Expose it, and it'll shrivel up in the heat. But there are different ways of saying. I learned this from my grandfather. He would say by the way he walked. He would say by the way he cut wood even when he'd grown old and his legs were bowed. He would say with his eyes, dark brown circles with centers of light, moons enormous and magnetic. He would say through his silent prayers and meditations. "The mountains speak," he'd tell me when I lived with him. I listen to them here in Thermal. From Los Duros, you can see them in the distance, shy, looking on, giving me courage. They say with silence. The wind's their voice. I sit in the hollow of the cave made by the overhang. There, the wind doesn't carry the smell of the dying Salton Sea. It's hot, always jumping, a thing of energy. If you listen, the mountain will talk. It tells me that I'm not forgotten. That I exist.

From the heights I can see Los Duros. It's not ugly from here. The hills roll under it, causing the shacks and trailers to rise and sink in waves. You can see the heat making the air go wild, the desert floor and its people vibrating. On Saturdays, when they burn the trash, I sit and watch from here. The flames rise but are almost invisible as their yellow tails join the sun. Only the smoke can be seen. It's a stain on the sky. The smoke says, "You're not so much. You will die. You will disappear. You can't hide." It drifts, hovering over the shacks and trailers. What happens to the smoke? I used to believe that it just went away, carried by the hot winds into nothing. Until Teacher showed me different. Now I know the smoke covers us all. It's the grimy surface of Los Duros.

The fire says too. I've been watching Los Duros burn. Today, after leaving Teacher's trailer, I walk back to my house. The dust is strong, choking me. Lots of the men are wearing bandanas over their mouths and noses. The little kids stay inside. But the mothers and fathers and the older kids are busy moving their small piles of things to the backs of old trucks. They're leaving before men with guns and badges come and make them. I walk into my house, my mother is lying on her mat, her face a sloppy pile of sadness. There is an empty glass next to an empty bottle turned on its side. The bottle is all out of what it has to say.

She won't wake up. Not until her body says that it needs more words from the bottle. If I stayed long enough, her tongue would come unstuck, her hands would say their pain to me, and the skin on my face would understand. But I'm not here to stay. I'm here to see the death of Los Duros.

The people will leave, like dry corn husks blown by the wind. María, a girl younger than me, also from Michoacán, but not Tarascan, is gone. She died. Her mother wanted her to stay so she could get treatment for her sickness. But she died anyway. She kissed me one time. The only time I've ever been kissed. I was outside and the sun had just dropped below the mountains, and the evening was cool. I'd only been here for a short time and she came to where I was standing and told me something about herself. Her name at first. That much I got. But the rest, I didn't. I couldn't tell her anything. I was too shy and I knew I would sound dumb. She smiled at me. She had long black hair as thick as the black wool yarn of a doll my mom once had. She came close to me, and before I could even move, she brought her head forward and kissed my lips. Then she ran. She didn't talk to me again and I stayed away. I miss watching her.

The burning goes on. It hasn't stopped. All that's changed is that they're making us leave. Los Duros isn't much, but it has its say too. It talks through the people who have learned to love each other here. It talks in the voices of the kids who play in the dust. It talks in the rattling coughs of old cars. You may not like what it has to say, but it isn't all bad. There's life here. It makes me sad. I don't like leaving places. I would like to stop moving, but the winds are too strong.

My mother doesn't move. I'm careful not to wake her. I'm quiet as I put some things in a plastic bag. There's no reason to come back. It'll all be gone soon and she's no better for having me here. At the entrance to Los Duros, I turn towards the shacks on the sandy paths. It'll get dark soon. I want to feel that I'm leaving for good. I know that I am, but I don't feel it until I see the blue peacock an old man keeps. He stands in the road, still proud, his head bobbing in search of something or someone. Maybe the old man left him behind. I watch him until I feel ready to leave.

When I get back to Teacher's trailer, he isn't there. Juan is sitting on the rose couch drinking beer. He cranes his head around, looking at me as he takes a long swig. He nods at me, "Grab a beer, I brought a twelve pack."

I put my bag down and take a beer from the refrigerator. "Where's Teacher?" I ask.

"Gone, *vato*. Wasn't here when I walked in."

"Did the police take him?"

"The cops were here?" he asks.

"Earlier."

"What did they want?"

"They think he started the fire."

"Fucking thing that fire," Juan says taking another drink. "A real fucking thing. Whoever did it should be given a gold medal. I'd've done it myself, if I would've thought of it."

"Why didn't you?"

"Think of it?" he says. "I don't know. Probably did think of it, maybe a million times only there's other things I'd burn the fuck down before the school. Shit, this whole desert ought to be burned up. Melt all the fucking sand into a clear glass sheet, all the people and houses and bricks and stone, melted right inside it like those bugs that get trapped in that lava shit."

"Amber," I say.

"Whatever. Just so long as they're trapped."

"Are you staying here?" I ask.

"For a while. No place else to go, homie, and the Teach, he's an alright guy. So I'm going to kick it here until he gets sent packing. They already fired him. Cops are already nosing around. It won't be long."

"You think that he did it?"

"Fuck, I don't know. Like I said, I woulda. I sure wouldn't blame him." He drains the can and pops another that's been sitting on the floor. "Nah, I don't think so. The Teach ain't no firebug. He's the type of motherfucker that'd sooner punch a sucker in the mouth than sneak in and burn his shit to the ground. Now, me?"

"You would?"

"Far as I'm concerned, there's a lot of shit that needs burning. There's a lot of motherfuckers that need shooting. There's a lot of loot that needs stealing."

He's drunk. His tongue's loose.

"You think they'll take him away?"

"Hell, if they can, bro, if they can. Haven't you been here long enough to know that yet? You're a *mojado*. You gotta know that's all they do. They use your ass up and then they ship you off. What do you think they're doing in Duros? Fuck, I'll be damned if they kick my ass out before I set my shit on fire. Hell, I'll throw a goddamn bomb in the fucker. I know a *vato*, a banger who had to join the army to stay out of jail. They taught that fool all the wrong shit. He don't give a fuck. He'll hook all kinds of shit up just for kicks."

The phone rings and Teacher's voice comes on telling the caller to leave a message. A man speaks slowly, "This is a message for Juan. I am looking for him. Tell him I'm looking for him." The phone goes dead.

"Is that your father?" I ask him.

"Yeah," Juan says. "Thinks he is, anyway, goddamn jailbird."

Teacher will leave. They'll make him. It doesn't matter if he set the fire. If my grandfather were still here, I'd ask him what all of this means. What I should do. Should I keep hiding? Teacher says no one should hide, that we can speak and act as one. He thinks that even the unheard can speak loud enough if we have courage. That's why I learn the computer and figure out the programs. María is still alive on the screen. It's a comforting bit of magic. I watch her again and again. These words and images that we put on the camera have made new trouble, maybe worse trouble. But I can watch María, who'll never come back. Only in the memory of that screen.

Juan leaves the trailer. Teacher is still gone. I sit outside in the shade in a broken chair Teacher found next to a Dumpster at the school. It's strong enough to hold me, but it's torn. A pickup drives up. A man in a cowboy hat and smoking a cigarette steps out. He takes a look at me, maybe thinking at first that I'm Juan. He takes a drag, the smoke pouring out of his nose and mouth and throws the cigarette on the gravel, crunching it with the toe of his black boot. He takes off his hat as he walks up to me.

"You live here too?" he asks.

I nod. He seems angry and scared.

"Juan's not here? You know—Banger?"

I shake my head.

"Don't talk much, huh?"

I don't say anything.

"I'm his father," he says. He reaches out to shake my hand. I give him mine and he shakes it loosely like he's being careful not to break an egg. "Been worried about him. You his friend?"

I don't answer because I don't know. I only know that Juan and me are brothers.

"Listen, do me a favor. I know you don't owe me one, but let Juan know that I need to find him and talk to him. I'm worried. I had police come to my house asking me if I knew where he was."

"You can wait here," I tell him. "He may come back."

The man looks around, maybe for a chair. There's only the broken one I am sitting on. He looks back at his truck. "Yeah, maybe I'll do that. I've been calling, but no one picks up. I'm going to sit over there," he says walking back to his truck. He lights another cigarette, and now sitting partly in the sun, puts his hat back on. The smoke continues to stream out of his nose and mouth joining in a small cloud that disappears into the air.

Teacher comes back a few minutes later. The father watches him step out of the car. Teacher walks towards the truck and nods at the father. They shake hands and walk back to the trailer. They're going to talk. Teacher gives me a nod and a pat on my shoulder as he passes by. When they walk in, shutting the door behind them, I crawl under the trailer.

"The police have been looking for Juan," the father says. "They've called four or five times and they sent a detective over a while ago. They seem to think that Juan might have something to do with this. You know anything?"

"Nothing," Teacher says. "My guess is that they're just trying to sweat you so that you'll do something that'll lead them to him. They're grasping at straws on this thing. It could've been anybody who set the school on fire. There's a lot of pissed off people in this town. Whites and Mexicans. It wouldn't surprise me if some of these good souls decided they'd set the place on fire so that they could get rid of all the Mexicans, not just the ones in Los Duros."

"You put them up to this?" the father asks.

"Put who up to what?"

"You know what I'm talking about."

"C'mon. That's a bad question. That's the kind of question the cops ask. They want to find easy answers to this thing. If they can't pin it on some poor kid, they come after me as an instigator, an outside agitator. All pure bullshit."

"Because these kids, they're in bad enough shape with all the things that are going on here without you getting in on it. Even if you think you're doing something good for them, you're not. You're too young to know yourself probably, but I'm not. It never pays to mess with these people."

"What people?"

"All of them. The *gabachos* with power, the *gabachos*

with no power. All of them got something to lose, something to protect and they don't want any goddamned Mexicans telling them how and where they draw the line."

"I'm sorry," Teacher says, "but I don't agree. I won't accept that we just have to shut up and either take it or go away."

"Look around," the father says. "Go down to Los Duros and see for yourself. The people there are going away. God knows where they're going, but they're going. And you can bet they don't like it. But they've got no choice now. I'd say you have something to do with that. But I'm not here to talk that out with you. I'm here to find my boy and do something before it's too late."

"Too late for what?" Teacher asks.

"Did he do it?"

"Do what?"

"Set the fire, goddamn it."

"Honestly, I don't know," Teacher says. "If you're asking me if I have knowledge of Juan committing arson, then the answer's no. But if you're asking me if he's capable of it? That's a different question. I don't know him well enough to answer that. Shouldn't you know better than me, sir?"

"You think this is a game," Juan's father says. "Maybe you think it's going to do something important, maybe change things. But it won't. I wish I knew my son like a father should. But I don't and that's my fault. But I know other things, things I've learned the hard way. All that you're doing is bringing more trouble for these people. The law will find someone to blame for this and for Juan or whoever, it's going to mean the end. We don't have a lot, but there's always more to lose. Maybe more than you think. I can't tell you about that. That's a question only a man can answer for himself. Tell my boy to call me when you see him. I have to talk to him. I've got to get to him before they do."

Teacher says, "Look, I'm sorry. I'm not here to cause trouble for anyone. I was just trying to help give these kids a say about something."

"Tell him to call me, or better yet, call me yourself when you see him. I don't want to hurt him. I'm trying to save him."

I hear Juan's father walk out. From below, I can see his black boots crunch in the gravel as he goes to his truck. My stomach feels sick because I know from my mother that there's no saving someone who wants to die.

§ § §

School goes on. There's yellow tape that says DO NOT CROSS POLICE LINE around the burned building. It makes everything smell like ashes. It's a scar now, black and gray, the roof falling down. The school isn't beautiful anymore. It's ugly like Los Duros, like the ugly, broken houses of Thermal and Mecca. It wasn't right anyway, that the school was perfect and untouched. All it did was remind us that outside the walls was sick and ugly.

I walk the halls listening. There's worried talk between the others, questions about where families will go, about the protest and whether it should still go on, about Teacher, about the fire. No one seems to know anything. They don't tell us anything here. In one class, a girl asks a teacher for the truth. But she doesn't answer anything. She says, "Don't worry about those things. Let Principal Joe and your parents worry. The police will find who did it."

No one here says anything worth hearing. I won't come back. When the others have begun to gather around at lunch, I walk towards the fence that surrounds the school. They lock the gate during the day so that no one can leave. There's a school policeman on a bike watching. He wears dark sunglasses so that we can't see who he's got his eye on. He watches with suspicion, believing that someone here set the fire and is planning something else. He doesn't know who, but he has his ideas. He looks like he wants to kill everyone.

I head for the small opening in the fence, and from behind I hear the policeman yell, "Hey, where do you think you're going?" When I don't stop, he yells louder, "Hold it right there! I'm talking to you, damn it!" But I don't stop. I can't stay here even a minute longer and he's shouting, his voice getting madder. I hurry now, because I'm suddenly sure that he's going to kill me, that he's going to take his stick and beat me until I disappear into the sand. I struggle at the opening. It's not big enough to walk through unless you make yourself small and turn sideways. Before I'm through, he's caught up to me on his bike. He jumps from the seat letting the bike fall to the sidewalk in a clatter, and he grabs my shoulders with his heavy hands. He pulls me backwards through the opening, and my head bangs against the metal post and I fall, my head hitting the sidewalk. He puts his knees on my chest, yelling for others to come help.

I don't struggle with him. I'm caught. No one can help me now. I hear more yelling and other guards have come. They pull me up, putting cuffs around my wrists, shoving me. Principal Joe comes running up, yelling, "What's going on here? What's the trouble?"

The policeman who stopped me tells him what I've done as the others lead me to Principal Joe's office. They put me in a seat in the hall outside the room. He comes in with the policeman and they walk inside and close the door. Another policeman stands with his back to the wall watching me. "You like burning shit, kid? Don't like it around here? Maybe you think it'd be better to set this thing on fire, huh?" I don't say anything to him. I watch him instead. He's a white man, young, stronger and bigger than the policeman who pulled me down at the fence. He's smiling at me but there's anger in his eyes. I know that look.

Principal Joe opens his door and says, "Bring him in." I stand up and walk to the door. The young policeman shoves me into the office. The other policeman is sitting against the wall. "Sit there," Principal Joe says pointing to the chair in front of his desk. He doesn't go around it to sit down. Instead, he sits on the corner of the desk on the same side as me.

"Where were you running to, son? Why didn't you stop when Officer Rodriguez told you to? It won't do you any good to stay quiet. We've got a decision to make. We can call in the city police, or you can tell us what's going on."

"You better talk, boy," the older policeman says.

I don't say anything. I sit there trying to keep quiet inside. I'm afraid, afraid like I get when my mother's drunk.

I can feel blood on my face from the scrape and there's a big lump on the back of my head. My shirt is torn and my face feels hot like I'm going to cry. But I can't in front of them. I try to think how my grandfather would act.

"Why were you running?" Principal Joe asks again. "Do you know something about this fire?"

"He did it," the young policeman says. "Sure as shit, he did it. Look at him. He's a classic firebug. Quiet and weird, textbook case."

"Is there any truth in that, son?" Principal Joe asks. "You don't have to lie anymore. If you did it, you might as well fess up and let us help you. It's going to be a lot worse later on. You got anything you want to tell us?"

I shake my head.

"Told you," the older policeman says. "He isn't going to tell us anything. These kids stick together, but he knows. He knows something."

"Weren't you in Mr. Peña's class?" Principal Joe asks. "I think I remember you in there. Makes sense that you're angry about him losing his job. Is that why you did it?"

I don't say anything.

"It's useless. Call the city police," Principal Joe says. "Let them handle it."

"What do we tell them he did?"

"Tell them he was attempting to leave school without authorization. Tell them that he resisted when you attempted to apprehend him. Tell them that you think he might know something about the fire."

§ § §

Teacher wants to know what happened. But I don't remember. It's like a dream, moments that fall in together like a roof collapsing. Juan's father, and Henry, the legless man who helped the Teacher a couple of times before the fire, in a white van. I remember that. They told Teacher that they found me wandering on the side of the road close to the Salton Sea. "He was just walking around looking like he'd just been drug through hell," Henry says to Teacher. "He's close to a heatstroke. I saw it every day in Iraq. He's damned lucky we found him. Another couple of hours in this heat and he'd been coyote food."

"Who did this to you?" Teacher wants to know. But I don't tell him because there's something coming for him, a jaguar hiding in the dark. It's set to tear him apart and I won't help the jaguar. What I can remember, I'll keep to myself because what's done can't be undone.

§ § §

The policemen came, two of them, both in uniforms. The one with the mustache didn't speak to me. The other one, the one whose lips curled up when he talked to me, took me by the collar, his thumb digging into the back of my neck where the school policeman had grabbed me and pulled me down. It hurt, but that's what he wanted. I kept silent. There was nothing to do but hold my tongue. Principal Joe told them, "He may know something about the fire. He's acting like he knows but doesn't want to say. We questioned him, but he's not going to talk to us. Maybe he'll talk to you."

It was hot, the waves of heat rising as we left the building. "You know something, big boy," the policeman with the sneer said as he pushed me inside the car. "You're going to tell us." He shut the door and walked around to the other side. The mustached policeman was already at the wheel.

"What do you think we ought to do with him?" the sneering man said.

The other one didn't look at him. "There's a lot we can do with him. What do you think?"

"Not going to take his ass to juvie, that's for sure. Not by a long damned shot. Let's take him out to the desert and do some questioning."

They pulled out on the highway that leads to the dunes. I could feel the heat through the window and my stomach tightened like it always does before. I tried to be quiet, to listen not to them, but to listen to my heartbeat. To keep calm. My grandfather taught me that. But I couldn't hear my heart. The policemen didn't say anything more. They drove into the desert, the dunes getting larger. The mustached policeman made a sudden turn and stopped the car, but left it running.

"Real hot out there, *chaca*. Real hot. You're going to give us someone, by god. You're going to give us the firebug. You can bet your ass that we're going to find the perp and I'm not about to let some sorry-assed wetback Indian, whatever the fuck you are, stand in the way of getting him."

The mustached policeman said, "That's right, son. You better come clean. Tell us what you know. I don't think it was you, but you got to give us something to go by. We know you're living with your teacher. Did he put you up to it? You can trust us. Just give us what we need and we'll take you home."

"He doesn't want to cooperate," the sneering policeman said. "I can tell just by the way he's hunched over back there. You think you're cool? Cool as a cucumber? It's not too fucking cool out there," he said. I said nothing. I kept my eyes focused on the dunes, on the sand blowing over the top, swirling down little by little, and reforming slowly.

The sneering policeman got out of the car and walked around to the back. He opened the trunk and then came to my side. He opened the door. The handcuffs were still on my wrists. He reached in and grabbed me by the torn collar of my shirt. "Get out here, goddamnit. Sweating balls out here, Kemosabe. Now I'm going to put you in a sweatbox. Probably won't work seeing as how you Indians like that sort of thing. Maybe a while in there will loosen that tongue of yours."

He pushed me to the trunk and said, "Get in." I didn't move and he shoved me hard from behind. "Get in, Kemosabe, or I'm going to put you in and I'm going to do it plenty rough." But it was hard because I couldn't use my arms. I leaned over the edge like I was peering inside. And then he kicked the back of my knees and as I began to fall, he pushed me into the trunk. He closed the lid. I heard him go back to his side of the car and get in.

It was dark in the trunk and I couldn't hear anything but muffled voices. I lay on my stomach, my hands behind my back, the heat of the sand coming up through the floor of the car. It burned and I tried to move on my side, but I couldn't turn. I began to breathe heavy, a fear that I was being buried. And then the heat, and something like a dream where my head banged against the roof of a shack, hard, making the sound of a fist banged on a table. And then my tongue so thick, and no water, not even spit, and my tongue hanging out like a dog. And then the itching of my scalp and neck and my arms behind me and then struggle and something like flames. Then blackness.

"You going to tell us, boy?"

"He doesn't hear you, Ray."

"He goddamn hears what he wants to hear. You going to give us some information? Or are you going back in that goddamned trunk."

"He's not going to tell you anything. You left him in there too long."

"Not long enough. You tell me what I want to hear."

Silence. And then kicked from behind, and the sand on my face and neck and then rolling in its fire.

"Pushing him down the dunes isn't going to do the trick. This kid probably doesn't even understand what you're asking. We ought to go back and haul that principal up here for wasting our time."

"He knows. Look at him. He fucking knows."

"He doesn't. He would've spilled it by now."

"He knows. He's not going to tell out of spite. Ain't that right, you spiteful little wetback?"

And then the sound of the car driving off through the sand and my hands free and feeling my wrists and then laughing and crying, one starting where the other finished, and then again and again. My tongue so thick, and no water, not even tears. And then the white van, and Juan's father and the legless man.

"Lucky we found you. It won't kill you, a heatstroke, not if you can get some water in time, but you'll feel like hell for a week."

And Teacher. "What happened? Who did this to you? Who took you out there?"

And my tongue thick in its cave, dry, blistered, but not saying anything except, "I won't help the jaguar."

"What are you talking about, jaguar?" Teacher kept asking.

"He doesn't know. He's out of his head," Henry told him.

§ § §

But it comes back in the same dream. At least I think it's a dream. My face on the burning sands, hot rocks and pebbles pressing into my skin, burned alive, but not so I turn black. I roll down the dunes, the grit in my eyes and mouth, rolling, rolling, until I come to a stop at the bottom, and then a giant jaguar at my feet, pawing at me, pulling me upwards with a sneer, and then a kick and a punch, and then rolling, rolling, until I stop, my face pointed upwards at the sun, its invisible flames swallowing me. The jaguar brings its fire. The jaguar says all it needs to say through fire. Who am I to stop him?

Teacher won't stop asking me what happened. He lets me sleep on his bed while he sleeps on the couch. Juan hasn't come around in days and no one, not Teacher or his father knows where he can be found. They think maybe I know. I hear them talk that night.

Juan's father says, "He did it. That's what it is. Now he's scared. He's run off."

Teacher says, "I don't think so, Juan. I don't think he did it. It doesn't make sense to me. Why would he set fire to my classroom?"

"Anger."

"What's he angry at? What's the story with you two?"

"No story, that's the problem," the father says. "You know him better than I do."

"How's that?"

"I did some things, got put away."

"Well, I don't know him that well. Juan doesn't talk much about himself."

"Anger and impatience," the father says. "In the joint, I lived with it. I saw it burn in everyone. I was lucky. I figured out that it burns everything it touches. It's got a hold of him now. He won't stop burning until he's destroyed himself."

"Anger's not all bad," Teacher says. "Sometimes it's necessary. I've tried to help these kids use their anger, direct it at someone, direct it for a purpose. It seems like you've done that."

"Anger isn't enough to keep you alive through ten years in a hole. I thought about other things. I thought about my son and how I'd make things different if I got another chance. Most of the *vatos* in the *pinta* talk about what they should have done different when they were on the outside. Regrets don't get you shit out here. You have to have something else. You have to put away the anger. You have to grow patience."

"So making things right with your kid, that's kept you going?"

Juan's father doesn't say anything.

Teacher says, "I know it's a scary thing. It seems like just saying it, just thinking about it, is enough to make it go away, enough to fuck the whole goddamn enterprise."

The father changes the subject. "What happened to the other boy? How bad is he?"

"Something bad. I'm not sure. I can't get a word out of him except for nonsense about helping jaguars. Hallucinating. Somebody took him out to the desert. Somebody worked him over."

"The cops think he did it."

"The fire? No, not that kid. I know him. He's quiet, works hard, never done or said a thing that caused anyone any trouble. I found him outside the principal's office a couple of months ago. Couldn't hardly speak any Spanish or English. He's a quick study though. He figured out the ins and outs of everything I've thrown at him. Tough case. His mom's an alcoholic. Domestic abuse. Tough. Add to that, he's a *chaca*."

"*Chaca*?"

"Yeah, Indian from the mountains, a Tarascan. The kids around here have to have someone to hate worse than they hate themselves, so they target the *chacas*."

I want to get out of the bed and tell them that there are no *chacas*. My grandfather was a village leader. He planted crops, fished, and hunted. He knew cures. What does that have to do with *chaca*? My grandfather would not have let the police take me to the desert. He wouldn't have let them take me by the neck and throw me down the dunes. He wouldn't have let the sneering policeman put sand in my mouth and eyes. He wouldn't have let the one with the mustache stand at the top of the dunes and watch. My grandfather wouldn't have let them. He would not have let them. And I feel the heat from my eyes, the salt burning, my mouth opening as if it wants to give voice to the moans inside, but I keep quiet. Like always.

§ § §

Juan comes in the night. He taps on the window of the bedroom. I look over because I can't fall sleep. I can hear Teacher snoring from the couch as I get up and go to the window. Juan is there, his face almost invisible because there's no moonlight.

"Where's the Teach?"

"Asleep," I say. "Where have you been?"

"Don't mind that shit right now. I'm in trouble, homie."

"How did you know I was in here?"

"I thought you were in the living room, but the Teach left the TV on and I could see that it wasn't you. I figured you were in here. Hey, what's the deal here? The cops come looking for me?"

"What did you do?"

"Nothing much, dude. Just threw *chingazos* with some white fucks who wanted to talk a lot of shit. Now with this fire thing, the pigs are looking for someone to pin it on. What the fuck happened to your face?"

"Nothing."

"Hell nothing. You get into a scrap?"

"Nothing," I say. "Nothing happened. Where've you been?"

"I saw the pigs came by my trailer in Duros. Fucking crazy over there. They're cleaning everyone out. I could tell the pigs got in and went through my shit. They're trying to pin this fire thing on me I think. That or those white boys we fucked up were some rich asshole's sons. Who knows? But I'm not stupid. Either way, I'm not showing up to find out."

"Your father's been here. Teacher is looking for you."

"I don't have a father. And I'm sorry about the Teach. But I'm not giving the fucking pigs a clear shot at me."

"What do you want?" I ask him.

"I need some help with something. There's something in it for you too. Maybe something in it for the Teach. Meet me outside."

I move quietly, but I'm slow because of the bruises on my legs and back. Teacher is a sound sleeper. His snores continue as I walk through the living room out the front door. Juan is sitting next to Teacher's truck, his back resting against the side.

"'Bout time, man. I thought you'd pussed out on me."

"What do you want?" I ask him again.

"Chill, man. Sit down. Let's work this thing out." I sit down. "Man, whoever worked you over did a good job. What happened?"

"The police," I say. I feel that I can tell him. That he will understand because he's my brother and because the jaguar's coming for him too.

"No shit," he says. "No fucking shit. They're after me too. *Puta madre*, they're after all of us, man. It's open season on Mexicans around here. I was over in Duros last night. Half the place is empty, a ghost town. And the other half is either too old to go anywhere or don't have a way of moving. The pigs have given them till the end of the week. Then watch out. They'll be there with their guns and pepper spray and a whole truck full of locks and chains. ICE too. Buses with one way tix to Mexicali and Tijuana."

"You said that you need my help, that you know how to help Teacher."

"I can help you too, bro. I need to get the fuck out of here. These bastards are fixing to try and send me to jail. I turn 18 in four months. That means that they're going to try me for aggravated assault. I could go to jail for six years."

"Can't anyone help you?"

"Like who? The Teach? Shit, he can't even help himself, Tarasco. It's cause of him that all this heat's down on us. Don't get me wrong. He was trying to help, but he shoulda known it would blow up in his face. Dude's toast around here. They fired him, right? And my father, he's a jailbird. You think that some judge is going to give him custody of me? He's an ex-con, a junkie motherfucker. No way. I'm not going to wait for them to send me up. And watch, they're going to pin this fire shit on somebody before too long. I've been around here long enough to know that it don't matter who pays, as long as someone pays."

"So what do you want?"

"My homie who just got deported, he had some

159

connections up in Mexico and another connect down here in Coachella. He was going to run some grass and some other shit down to Indio. Some *pelones* dropped it off for him. He was keeping it for a few days. People are waiting for their shit. If we take it to them, we make a good score. Enough to get me to Arizona. I got a cousin out there who'll give me a place to stay. I'll cut you in 50/50."

"How does that help Teacher?"

"Man, with me splitting into thin air, you tell the pigs that I told you I did it. That takes the heat off of the Teach. You gotta know he probably did that shit, right?" Juan's face is in shadow, but I can see his teeth and the whites of his eyes. He looks as if some dull light is coming from inside, a pale yellow glow like an orange moon.

"Teacher didn't do anything," I say.

"C'mon man. He's a fucking revolutionary. Of course he did it. And I'm fucking glad he did it. As far as I'm concerned, someone ought to strike a match to this whole goddamn desert, burn all this shit right down with all the people and their fucking golf clubs and all that bullshit. Kill 'em all, bro. I don't give a fuck. But I'm just saying, the cops aren't stupid. They're after you, they're after me, they're after the Teach."

"But he didn't do anything."

"That don't matter, fool. Of course he did something. Whether it was the fire or not, that doesn't matter. He came down here and disturbed shit. That's what he did. Whether it's the fire at the school or the fire inside, either way, these motherfuckers don't like it. And they're going to pin the shit on him whether he did it or not. Because one way or another, he's responsible. Get it? He either lit the flame himself, or he worked one of these *mojados* up enough to do it. He struck the match and he's going to pay. Unless."

"Unless I help you."

"Yeah, that's right. It's a good plan. I take the fall for it. I disappear. You take a cut and do whatever you want. Aren't you from the mountains or something? You could take off, get there in a couple of days and have enough *feria* to take care of your mom or whatever."

"What do you want?"

"What do I want?" Juan asks, his voice excited and impatient now. "I want to get the fuck out of here before I kill someone or someone kills me. All I need is some wheels, a lookout to help me get out of Duros without the cops getting me, and someone to ride shotgun to make the exchange. Then we split the money and we go our own ways. You tell the cops that I confessed the whole thing to you and that I took off for Mexico. They'll believe it."

"Why don't you get one of your friends?"

"Can't trust them, man. They're soft. They're punks. But you've got balls. I know that. You're always watching shit. You keep your mouth shut. You've got lots of shit you could snitch about, but you never have. Plus, you don't have any real connections here. You can pick up and go. You got as much at stake in this as I do. And I know you want to help the Teach." He stops talking. He's waiting.

"Where do we get a car?"

"I know where my old man keeps his keys. Saw them hanging on a hook at his place. He drives that van for the *mojados*, you know. He drives them to the showers.

Anyway, they park it at the Center where he works. I can take the key from the house and we hustle over there, drive the van down to Indio, make the exchange, and then we're back before the sun comes up. Long before the sun comes up, bro. And then we're home free."

I don't say anything.

"You aren't scared are you? I didn't figure you for somebody that gets scared. Anyone with the balls to come across the border and deal with all the shit that *chacas* get at school and on the streets, is someone I figure can deal with their nerves. Look, think about it tonight. But we gotta move quick. I'm talking by tomorrow night. Those fuckers are getting real *nervioso* about their smack. We don't want them coming down here for it either."

I'm done thinking. Either this is the way the jaguar will come, or it's the only way to escape him. There's no real choice.

"I'll meet you tomorrow night."

"Where?"

"In front of the store in Thermal."

"Tell the Teach that you're going home to see if your moms needs some help. He'll buy that and that way he won't suspect anything." He stands up and gives me his hand to help me get on my feet. "Good shit, man," he says. "Tomorrow, *vato*." He leaves, disappearing into the dark sands.

§ § §

I tell Teacher that I have to see my mother. "You need

a ride there?" he asks me. "No," I tell him. It's an excuse to disappear for the night, but it's true. I do need to see her. I walk to Los Duros. Juan was right. The dirt streets are empty, the dust blown into thick brown clouds kicked up by the rush of the people leaving. I find my mother's house. The screen door's broken, the spring that brings it back bent by the force she must've used leaving. Everything's gone, everything important.

She's taken her bedroll and mat. There are no dishes left except for some old plastic cups from hamburger places. She left the mat I sleep on, but she's taken the blankets. There's a pile of garbage in the kitchen, empty bottles and dirty paper plates with half-eaten beans and dried rice. My mother didn't have many clothes, but what she has, she's taken with her. Maybe she's waiting somewhere for me, but I don't think so. The time I've been at Teacher's, she's never tried to find me or ask about me at the school. There's no note because she can't write. Maybe she left word with the neighbors, but their trailer is empty too. There isn't much else, some old pieces of furniture too big to take on the run.

This is a sign. I sit on the wooden porch of the trailer and look down the empty street. Only the stray dogs seem to be left. I try to think what my grandfather would say. Nothing comes until I understand that I must have more sense than the stray dogs. You're a fox, my grandfather would tell me if he was here, not a dog.

Juan's waiting where he said he'd wait. He's in the white van that his father and the legless man, Henry, took me to Teacher's after the policemen had finished with me.

163

He looks small inside it. "Get in," he tells me as I walk to the door. He pushes it open, reaching across the wide front seats. He's jumpy. "C'mon, man, we gotta roll. We don't want to be sitting with some big motherfucking spotlight on us." I get in and close the door.

"What do we do?" I ask.

"We're going to Duros. I need you to stay behind the wheel while I go into my trailer and get the shit. Don't do anything stupid. Just sit there while I go in and out. You're just there to make sure no one's watching or following me inside. You see anything funny, you give the horn a blast. Just lean on it and then drive the fucker down the road, in that direction," he says pointing east. "Just about a mile and I'll catch up to you. But nothing like that's going to happen. I'm going to get in and get out. Then we head up to Indio. You do know how to drive, right? They got cars down in chacaland?"

"I can do it," I say.

"Alright, homie. That's all I want to hear."

We get to the entrance of Los Duros and Juan shuts off the headlights. We creep down the dirt streets silently, Juan looking and listening as if he is being hunted. "That's it," he says pointing out the window. "Right there. Looks just like I left it." He stops the van a few plots away from where his trailer stands. He leaves the van running. "Okay, I'll be right back." He's wearing black, a dark baseball cap pulled low over his face. It's a dark night and he disappears into its blackness.

I sit and wait. From far away, I can hear a dog wailing, maybe for his master who's gone. I wonder where my mother is. She didn't leave anything behind. This idea comes to me strong, this idea that I wouldn't allow myself to think about when I was in the trailer. I realize that I have to decide if I'll look for her.

I lose track of things when Juan jumps into view. He's carrying a cardboard box. He opens the passenger door and puts the box on the seat behind him. "C'mon, bro, let's move."

I put the van into drive and head towards the entrance.

"Got it," Juan says. "Fuck, I was a little worried, bro, I don't mind telling you. With the pigs looking through my shit the other day, and with my old man and the Teach, I was starting to think someone might get to this before I could. But I've got my hiding spots. Lucky too, because it would've been over, man."

"Why?"

"You think the people that sent this shit over here are just going to let their product disappear? That dude that set this shit up, he's probably wearing a Colombian necktie by now. Nah, man, I need to deliver this shit not just for the dough, but to make sure I don't wind up with my balls in my mouth in some dumpster." He reaches back for the box. "You aren't scared are you?"

"No," I say.

"Be scared just enough so you don't fuck up."

"What's in the box?" I ask.

"The shit I need to deliver and a couple of other things," he says. I look over at the box and see that sticking out from the top is a blue peacock feather.

"What's that?"

"Something my moms gave me before she died. It's a long story." By the dim light from the dashboard I can see that there is a picture of Juan and his mother. Juan is a little boy, his hair long, his mother, a short woman, holds his hand. They must be facing into the sun because young Juan is holding his hand up to shield his eyes.

The highway is empty, only a few big trucks on the road. The trains are running though, and I can hear their distant calls. When my mother and I came here, we took a bus to Mexicali and then went around the fence by foot. A *coyote* led us into the desert. It took three days to get here and I worried that we wouldn't make it, that the *coyote* would leave us to die in the hot sand. But when I heard the trains, I began to feel better, to believe that we were close to our new home.

"Did you find your moms?" Juan asks. He is driving now.

I shake my head.

"Did she split?"

"She's gone," I say.

"No note, nothing?" Juan turns on the radio. "I wouldn't worry too much, homie. She's sure to be in town somewhere. Where the hell's she going to go? Duros people are just going to crowd into another goddamn slum somewhere in Mecca. She's out there. You'll find her."

"No," I say. "I'm not going to look."

Juan doesn't say anything for a minute. He fiddles with the radio until he finds a station playing *rancheras*. "Hell, my moms is dead and I still look. Look every goddamned day."

This surprises me. "But your father," I say. "What about him?"

"Don't call him my father. He's a fuckup. I got no use for him. If he'd been around instead of being locked up, my moms would still be alive. She died waiting for that motherfucker."

"You'll die looking for your mother," I say.

"What does that mean? You say weird shit sometimes, *chaca*."

"Sometimes the fox says things I don't understand," I say after a minute.

"Fox? What the fuck you talking about? You 'shrooming on me? Keep your shit together until this deal is through."

Juan doesn't understand yet, so I keep quiet.

After a while, he stops at a gas station and makes a call from a pay phone. He talks for only a minute or two. He hangs up and comes back to the van. "This shit's intense," he says to himself so I can hear. "Look, these fools are serious, okay? So when we get there, don't come out with any of this fox shit or any other kind of *chaca* magic. Just do what you do best. Be big and quiet. I'll do the talking. It won't take long."

We turn off the highway a few miles outside of Indio. There aren't any streetlights and Juan strains looking at signs. He has never been here before. He's afraid of getting lost. "Goddamn it," he says from time to time, slowing the van, putting his brights on and sticking his head out the window as he decides which way to turn. We are climbing higher towards the mountains, driving the wandering course of a small desert road.

"I think this is it," he says. He parks the van and flashes the lights on and off three times. And then from a distance, his signal is repeated. Headlights blink on and off. "I've got a piece," he says to me as we watch a truck approach slowly, like a cat creeping up on its prey. He pulls a gun from his waist. "I'm going to put this motherfucker on the seat. I'm letting you know in case, bro, just in case. You stick to the van and if you see any crazy shit go down, you know where it is."

The truck comes closer until I can make out that it is white, new, heavy with big tires and a front end that looks like a sneer. "Be cool, now," Juan says to me as he steps out. "When I say, you bring me the package in the box. But not till I say." The truck drives up to the front of the van so that both vehicles are nose to nose. The lights come on suddenly, the white glare hitting me in the eyes. I shield my face with my hand. I can't see the driver or the passenger or if there's anyone in the backseat. I'm blinded.

Juan moves slowly, leaving the van door open as he approaches the truck.

The passenger door opens and a figure steps out. Juan stops and I hear someone talking in broken Spanish. He's telling him not to move, to show him his hands. He wants to know who I am. He wants me to step out of the van. Juan tells the men that I'm his cousin and one of them says that he doesn't care who I am. Juan says, "Cool it. He's a dumb *chaca*. He's not from here."

"I don't care if he's from Mars. You both look illegal to me. Tell him to show me his hands and get his ass out here." Juan looks back at me. He looks confused.

"Hey, who are you guys?" he asks.

"That's a good question, fella, that's a good question. But we're more interested in who you are and what you're doing so close to the border in a van this late at night."

Juan cocks his head back at me.

"You hold it there," the figure says, "you just hold it." I can't make out his face yet because of the light in my eyes. "You stay exactly where you are. We're armed. You show us your hands in there. We're calling the Border Patrol and we'll let them sort this whole thing out. Victor," he says, "put in the call. Now you, the one in the van. You come out of there slow, big boy. Show us those *manos. Comprende*?"

I grab the box with my left hand, the gun with my right and when I slide around the van, I put it in my back pocket. I walk out between the van and truck, the headlight shining in my face for a moment before I move into the dark.

"What's that?" the voice asks when he sees I'm holding the box.

"Hey, you don't know what you're fucking with," Juan says.

"I'm pretty sure I know," the voice says.

"No you don't, *culero*."

"Just drop it," the voice orders. I drop the box in the sand. "You keep an eye on this one while I check it out, Victor," he says. The man behind the wheel steps out.

The voice creeps up, keeping his eyes on us. He bends down to pick up the stuff that's fallen out. The box is upside down. Just a feather and some other stuff," he says.

"Check it all out," Victor says.

"There's something else here," the voice says. "Oh shit,

Victor, oh shit. There's something in here alright. Drugs I think. It's got to be drugs. We got ourselves something here, Victor, something big."

Juan is standing there, his shoulders narrowing in his anger and fear. "You don't know what you're doing. The fuckers this shit belongs to are gonna be here and then you're going to see."

"Shut up," the voice says. "Shut up, *vato*." He says *vato* all wrong, probably somebody from up north, somebody who learned his Mexicans from TV. Juan jumps at him, and Victor, who's walked up to see the box, notices and faster than I could've imagined slices at him, like a dark blade, the gleam of metal flashing for a split second in the headlight. It's brighter than anything else in the desert, and then I see Juan's hands at his face, and he makes a moan and falls to the sand. This all happens so fast that I don't think about pulling the gun out of my pocket. It just is. It's out, in my hand, but not my hand, and I pull the trigger and there is a flash of orange, and for a split moment, everyone's face is bright, and I see the voice's teeth, white and sharp, a jaguar's fangs turning towards me as his comrade falls to the sand without a sound, without another motion. And without waiting for the jaguar to strike, I point and feel myself squeeze the trigger, this time deliberate, and then again. Victor has crawled to the truck but he can't pull himself up. In the headlight's arc is Juan, still on his knees, picking up the box with one hand, the other at his mouth where the blood has seeped down his neck and shirt. Victor and the voice are perfectly still now, revealed as men for just another moment until I hear Juan curse loudly.

I pick him up by the arm. "Let's go," I say.

"Grab that shit," he says pointing at the package of powder.

"No," I say, and I pull him away. "Let's go. Now."

"You're crazy." And he pulls out of my grasp and bends down again, this time for the drugs. "Help me," he says. I pull him to his feet without letting him pick it up. He is weak, his knees have no strength and the blood seeping down the front of his shirt and pants now, a red stream mixed with saliva and tears, streaks down my bare arm. I push him into the back seat of the van. Then I throw his box with the feather and the picture in the front. I run around the van to get in. I pull backwards, keeping my eyes on the two figures, one dressed in green, the other in black. The voice in black moves, his hand twitches, his mouth is open in a big O as if he is trying to say something at the ghost that killed him.

"C'mon," Juan says from the backseat, "before the cops."

I keep pulling backwards, the arc of light broadening on the scene. "Green and black, green and black," I repeat in my head as we speed away, the sand wanting to keep us there. From the back, I hear Juan throw up.

"Jesus, fuck, man, where'd they come from? Why'd you shoot him? It's all fucked up, man, all fucked up," Juan keeps saying. He takes off his bloody T-shirt and rips it along the seam, wrapping it around his mouth and cheek, trying to stop the bleeding. "Goddamn, I'm bleeding like a pig. Jesus," he says again. "Where you going? Don't go this way. We gotta go another way. We can't just get on the highway, Jesus, man. There's probably a whole crew of ICE motherfuckers on their way. They're all going to be looking for us. Christ," he says.

The lights of 18-wheelers from across the highway shine into the van, white sheets of light passing over my face, my hands, the wheel, the back seat, where Juan is lying stripped to the waist, splotches of drying blood streaking his chest and stomach. He keeps moaning and the smell of his blood and vomit, copper and acid, carry up front to where I sit.

"Those motherfuckers are dead, *ese*, they're dead. We're dead. Either the cops are going to do it or those Mexicans are going to come after us. Why'd you leave the *chiva* there? That was stupid."

I don't say anything. I replay it in my mind, like a movie I'm editing for Teacher, and I see the yellow face of the voice in the shower of light from the gun and then another pull of the trigger, and the terrific sound of it swallowed by the darkness of the desert so quick, like it never happened.

"We gotta disappear," Juan says. "We gotta disappear fast. Can't go back to Thermal. They'll be there tonight or tomorrow."

But I'm not running. I'm going back to Thermal. Where else is there to go? My grandfather is dead. My mother is gone. Teacher? I keep driving down the highway. Juan's quiet, weak from the blood. He moans, but he doesn't say anything more. I look down at my hands, tight around the steering wheel, covered in sticky, drying blood. I want to wash them. That's when I notice that I'm covered with blood, the front and back seats of the van are streaked with blood. There's blood everywhere. I want to close my eyes, but instead, I drive.

It's still dark when I pull in front of Teacher's trailer. Juan's asleep or maybe unconscious. I need to think, but I don't want to think. I step out of the van and walk towards the door. The air is cold on my face, the wind picking up, blowing me forward. I knock loudly before I change my mind and walk away from everything. I hear Teacher's footsteps, loud and clumsy, a man still asleep. He opens the door and says, "Jesus, what's happened?" He steps out and looks at the van parked on the gravel. I've left the driver's door open and it looks abandoned. "What did you do?" he asks again.

"Juan's in there," I say.

"Juan?" Teacher walks out in his bare feet. He looks into the van and says, "Christ, what have you two done?" I haven't moved, and he says, "Come here and help me get this kid out." I walk up and Teacher already has Juan propped up, his right arm under Juan's shoulder. He pulls him out, Juan moaning. "C'mon, boy, help me." And the two of us carry Juan inside. We put him on the couch, and Teacher says, "We gotta get this kid to the hospital." Juan moans, "no," and I can't find any words.

"You gotta tell me, Tarasco, what happened?"

But I can't say anything. He goes to the telephone and dials, "Juan, it's Guillermo, something bad's happened. You need to get over here. Your son's here and he's in bad shape. I don't know, I don't know. Yeah, we'll be here." And he hangs up.

He covers Juan with an Indian blanket and slowly pulls the torn T-shirt from Juan's face. It sticks to his wound, a long slice from Juan's mouth to the bottom of his eye.

There's a thick brown crust that oozes with thickened blood. He goes to his bathroom and comes out with iodine and a bowl filled with warm water and a towel. He says, "Go get out of those clothes. Wash yourself up, do it quick. And bring those clothes with you when you get out. Hurry, now."

I go and strip off the clothes. In the mirror of the bathroom, I look at myself naked. The blood looks like war paint and there is a red handprint on my neck. I'm looking at a strange twin. I stand in the tub and the blood rinses off in the hot water, turning it pink as it mixes and makes a stream against the white. Steam rises in front of me, and my twin disappears in the mirror. The water scalds me, and the blood is replaced with the redness of burning flesh. It gives me something to feel so I don't move for a long time until I hear the front door slam shut and hear Juan's father saying something loud and then Teacher's voice loud, but calmer. And then he knocks loudly on the bathroom door, "Come out here, Tarasco, hurry."

I step out and put on clean clothes, grabbing the bloody ones in one hand. I walk into the living room, where Juan's father is squatting beside his son, a small wet towel in his hand. It has turned pink and red. He looks up at me, Teacher standing behind him. "We have to know what happened, kid. You've got to tell us right now."

But I still can't say. Juan's father stands up and comes towards me. He grabs me by the shoulders, "What were you two doing?"

Juan finally says, "It went wrong."

"What went wrong?"

"The deal. We were just supposed to drop off a package."

"What kind of package, goddamnit?" says the father.

My body's shaking now and I feel cold even though my flesh is still hot. I feel dizzy and I sit down in a chair. The father stands there.

"We should get him to the hospital," Teacher says.

"No," the father says. "We can't do that. We'll take care of this."

Teacher says, "That's not a good idea."

"We'll deal with it," the father says. "Goddamn it," he says again, rubbing his thick hand through his sweaty hair. They go outside and through the window, I can make out the two of them pulling a hose to the van, Juan's father opening the doors while Teacher sprays the inside. The father comes back in to grab a sheet and some towels.

When they finish, Juan's father drives off in the van and Teacher comes back in. "Listen, kid, sit down. Let's get things straight. I want to know what happened."

"Juan wanted to leave. We were going to leave."

"Where?"

"Home," I say.

"Christ," he says. "Who did this?"

"One of them. They were in the shadows."

"What're you talking about? Get it together. Here," he says and he gets up and pours me a glass of whiskey. "Drink this, drink it fast." I drink the brown liquid. It burns, making me feel less cold. "I know you're freaked out. But you have to collect yourself. You've got to talk. What happened?"

4.

Some noise about the Santa Ana winds and fires blowing across the state, a firestorm. That's what I hear. That's most of what I remember. The newsman talking about the drought and how people's houses are getting burned to the ground. I feel hot, my face is burning and I bring my hand to my cheek and it's swollen and cracked. I try to get up because I gotta piss, but I can't move and I'm going to piss myself. Tarasco is sitting in front of me, his big stupid face watching and it comes back to me, the sound of the gun going off twice, and the motherfucker who cut me falling in front of me, his chin and mouth half-buried in the sand in a howl frozen in ugly yellow. Laugh now, motherfucker, laugh now. "I gotta piss," I tell the *chaca*. "Help me get there." He lumbers over and gives me a hand. He has to stand next to me while I leak. I look in the mirror while I piss. There's a bandage wrapped around my cuts. It covers my face from just under my eye to my mouth. I look like a *pinche* mummy.

Even though I'm hurting, I don't moan, not in front of Tarasco, not in front of anyone. There's no use crying.

Like when my mother got killed by a *pinche indio* drunk off his ass coming out of the casino she worked at. She'd just gotten done with her shift and she's driving home, when the *indio* ran a light and pile drove her old piece of shit Fairmont. She died slow. Bled to death while they tried to cut her out of the wreck. I don't think about it much. Like I said, why sit around and moan about things that you can't do anything about? Now, the things you can do something about....

"What's going down," I ask Tarasco. He stands there, still quiet, his mouth tight as a pussy. "Hey, you with me? Wake up, homie. Who knows what?"

"Teacher knows. Your father too."

"Fuck. Where's the van? Did they take the smack?"

"I left the drugs in the desert. And they cleaned the van. Your father drove off in it. Teacher followed."

"Goddamn, man. The cops aren't going to be far behind. That fucker who called it in probably gave them a license plate or something. And that's not even the worst of it. There's the others, the ones who were coming for the *chiva*. You think they're going to let this thing lie? They know who I am. It won't be shit for them to come down and find out where I live, where my old man lives." On the television, there's some *gabacho* standing in front of a hill that's on fire, the flames and smoke fighting, the smoke winning and rising in the air away from the yellow tips of the blaze. The *gabacho* is saying, "The inferno is growing hotter and moving faster than they can fight it." I watch it for a second, the fire in the room like it's going to scorch us through the glass. "You get hurt?" I ask Tarasco.

He shakes his head.

"Because we're going to have to cut out of here. The Teach, my pops, no one's going to be able to help us with this shit. Only thing to do is get going."

"Where is there to go?" the *chaca* asks.

"Some mountain in Mexico, or Canada, or the fucking ocean, hell, I don't know. Somewhere far where those Mexicans and the *pinche chota* won't think it's worth following. What happened to the piece?"

"The gun?"

"Hell yes, the gun. Man, you have to wake up. I can't be slowing down all the time. I can barely move and you're going to have to keep up, at least till we get out of this place. I need to get back to Duros. I need to get out of here. Who knows what the Teach or my old man is going to do? They might decide it's better to go to the cops or some stupid shit like that. Goddamn, man, we got caught slipping." I look over at Tarasco. He's in a daze, his eyes open but looking like someone hypnotized him, like maybe he's seeing the shit that went down last night over and over again, like some crazy loop. "You listening to me?" I say to him.

"I left the gun in the van. You didn't kill anyone," he says.

"You think anyone's going to believe that? You think they're interested in who exactly pulled the trigger? Two Mexicans killed two motherfuckers. And then there's the drugs. Nah, man, there ain't no innocent bystanders in this." He stands there looking loopy as hell. "Hey, any of your people still up in the mountains? You got somewhere we can go to? Some relatives?" I say.

"It's a long way. I don't remember the way anymore," Tarasco says.

"There's maps, *vato*. Help me up. Let's get out of here before they get back and try to stop us." I reach out my hand to him and he pulls me up. "You got anything you need to take?" I ask him.

"Some clothes."

"Well, get them. We have to get moving."

On the television they cut from the fire to a sheriff who describes the murder of two Minute Men. "We're investigating the shootings. We believe the crimes are drug-related. That's all for now," the sheriff says as reporters ask him questions.

Motherfucking *putos*. Amateurs sticking their noses in shit that's got nothing to do with them. Fucking glad Tarasco blasted them. "Let's blow," I tell the *chaca*. But I can't stand too well, so I have to put my arm around his shoulders to get moving.

My old man's truck is out there, but there's no keys. Duros is at least five miles. We're going to have to walk it. "Get some water together," I tell Tarasco. "As much as you can carry. We're going to have to go across the dunes. Can't take a chance on walking the streets, not the way I look."

He's game. I think he's one of them old school *indios* like you see on the Discovery Channel, the one's who do the rain dances and shit. The ones like that movie *A Man Called Horse* I saw once where they take this dude and hang him up by his nipples with fish hooks to see if he can take the pain. I bet Tarasco saw some shit like that. Maybe he's done shit like that. The way he pulled the trigger last night, goddamn, bang...bang, like nothing. I didn't see it coming. No matter how you plan shit, no matter how you do, sometimes you get caught slipping. So homie had my back, but what now? I know they aren't going to just forget about this. We killed two Deputy Dog motherfuckers. Left them there on the hot sand for some coyote to drag off. At least Tarasco finished the job.

This wasn't supposed to happen. Me and my crew ran some shit through the school, nothing big. Mostly *mota* for the *sureños* who work the fields. Sometimes if Oscar got his hands on some *coca* or meth, we'd sling it, but nothing heavy. It was Oscar who had some cousin's crime partner tell him that he could make some good *feria* just doing the go-between shit. He'd only done it twice. I didn't even get involved, only held it for him in my trailer since there was nobody there to snoop. Now it's coming for us hard. If it isn't the cops, it'll be the Mexicans whose *chiva* we were supposed to deliver. I'm more afraid of them than the cops. They'll cut our balls off while we watch.

Tarasco is quiet. He never talks much, always alone except for the Teach. I used to see him in Duros, him walking around with his hands in his pocket, a big slow-walking fucker. Before I met him, I thought he was slow in the head too. His moms lived not too far. She was little and dark, a hard-nosed *india*. None of them people are too friendly. They keep to themselves, though. They don't want problems.

I never thought too much about Tarasco, only noticed him when the Teach came to Desert Mirage and started gathering his own crew of fuckups and misfits. Tarasco, like all the other kids, took the Teach's shit serious. Thought that maybe the revolution would come and shit. Maybe I did for a second till they fired him just so us Mexicans would get the message loud and clear: you don't fuck with the Man. At least, not straight up. You find the angles, the cracks, and you make sure you don't get caught.

The question I didn't ask myself when the Teach was talking his Zapata revolution shit was, "Why do I care what happens in this motherfucker?" This goddamn desert already took my moms, took my friends one at a time, takes your sweat and your blood, even your piss, spit, and come, and doesn't give anything back. I should've stuck to the plan. Make good for yourself even if you've got to slap someone down to do it. Traveling with a group just makes you a bigger target. Run on your own or with a tight crew, that's what works if you want to stay out of jail or the box.

The way I see it now, the Teach is a sucker. All the shit he talked about telling our story got us zip. He turned us into half-pint snitches blowing the game the Sanchez-Portillo Indians had going burning all that polluted shit, and got us all the wrong attention. Then these motherfucking politicians come down and then their gangs come riding in, the Minute Men and the ones with badges and guns. And now here I am, fucked up, walking these burning sands with this crazy *indio*.

"Gimme some of that water," I tell him. He hands me a two-liter bottle. The water is hot like coffee, but it'll do in this heat. We sit down for a minute on some rocks. There's no shade, but I have to slow down a little because my head is spinning. The sweat stings my cuts so I take a handful of water and wash out the wounds as best I can. The bloody clots dissolve in my hands and the cut alongside my eye starts to bleed again. Tarasco looks at me for a second and then back in the direction we're walking. "Smoke," he says pointing at the sky.

Sure enough, smoke, black streams of it rising from Duros, four or five pillars coming together high in the air in a gray cloud hovering like a flock of buzzards.

"Maybe we should stay away from there," he says.

"We can't. I've got some money stashed. Not a lot, but enough to get us some bus tickets, enough to get us out of here, maybe as far as your mountains down south. You got any other ideas? We can't sit around at a Denny's till we figure it out." As usual, Tarasco doesn't say anything.

In the old days, when we needed money, me and my crew would roll out to the casinos on the weekend and smack some sucker. You should see them coming in and out of the casinos every night. These *pinche indios* get them drunk so they'll keep feeding the slots and dropping their paychecks off at the table. They rob them inside and we rob them outside. Mostly, it was easy. People just hand you their money. The worst it ever got was when we gave this slacker asshole a beatdown once. He and his girl were down from L.A. and they were headed to their car across the parking lot where it was dark and empty. I bet he didn't want to get it scratched. He was drunk as hell and his chick was trying to keep him steady, talking about he should give her the keys. He was arguing in a little pussy voice and as soon as they got on the driver's side, we struck fast. It's got to be fast and I was pumped.

She saw us before he did and she said, "Daniel," all scared. "Hey, hey, wait, hey," the dude started screaming. Flea smoked his ass with a right cross and his girl, she just held her hand out with the keys saying "please, please" and I thought, don't you know it's too late for that? Now the dude was on his knees, still screaming. Oscar grabbed hold of his hair and slammed his head into the side of his bullshit Volkswagen. He went down hard and I grabbed his pant pocked and ripped that shit right off his ass, his wallet came out on the pavement and we took it and ran. The whole thing lasted twenty seconds. I don't remember what we got, but it wasn't enough.

But ain't that always the case? It's like when I was a kid, and my mother would tell me that when my father came back, that we'd go somewhere else, somewhere better. He never did come back and she kept waiting until the day she died. I believed it too until there wasn't nothing left to believe. In no time, I learned that the only thing you can count on about humans is that they all got stinky feet and itchy assholes. Ain't nothing that lasts, not love, not loyalty, not no fairy tales about Jesus and his crew of angels coming to the rescue. I guess if I've got anything to thank my old man for, it's that much. He taught me that waiting is for suckers. That's where the Teach gets it wrong. He believes the fairy story that if you get enough people to care, that things change. He didn't grow up in the desert or else he'd know that this is no place to keep things alive, especially belief.

Take Duros--there's two types of shacks. There's the shack where everything has gone to shit. Broken windows, old tires in front, trash piled up, the joint looking like no one lives there even though there's probably six or seven people. And then there's the place where *mamacita* or *abuelita* keeps a garden going, maybe a rose bush or some other kinds of plants. No running water, but they still find enough to keep the *matas* alive. Shitty thing, but they're the ones who don't last. The desert is good for killing what doesn't belong.

After about two hours, we come up on the hill overlooking Duros. It looks like the firebugs got here over the past few days. Dozens of charred trailers, smoke and soot still cloud the air. There's a three-legged dog walking one of the dirt roads. A car drives by and he hides underneath a battered dusty heap with flat tires that some *mojado* never did get running. More busted hopes. See that, Teach? One day you're wondering how you got here and you're planning how you'll get out, and the next, someone's pushing you out at the point of a gun.

We're being dodgy, looking around, trying to see if someone's watching for us. But it's a ghost town for the most part. There's a few stragglers, people who have no way to get out, maybe because they're too old, or have babies and no man. There are signs posted at the entrance saying that the place is being closed. My trailer is still standing, and the sheriff's been around to stick a notice on the door that my dead moms has been evicted. It doesn't even make me mad. It's almost funny. Wonder if they'll dig her bones up and scatter her in the desert. "There's No Room Here for Mexicans," the signs might as well say. Fuck 'em.

I don't have a key so we go around back and Tarasco

climbs in a window. He comes around and opens the door. I walk in. The place is a wreck. Someone's been here since I came for the dope. The place is ransacked to hell and back. The few things that were in there are either missing or tossed in the middle of the floor. Tarasco stands there, big and dumb, watching the way he always does. "Hey, *mi casa es su casa*," I tell him. I laugh at this but he doesn't.

I leave him there and walk back to my mother's room. I decided when my mom got killed that I'd shut the door to her bedroom and I wouldn't open it anymore. That was my way of saying I'm shutting all this out. It was like a symbol. I stand outside the door. I've got to go in because she had a little box she kept some emergency cash in. I'd put it in my hiding spot behind the wall. I never did touch it because it was like some good luck charm or something. She was still watching over me. Stupid. I walk in and of course it's gone. Everything is gone. Her small bed, the broken down dresser where she kept the few clothes she had. I should've known. Maybe I did, but with everything, I wasn't paying attention. I sit against the wall and put my head in my hands. It hurts more now, maybe the heat or the walking, but it's more than the cuts, more than a headache. It's like my last idea has finally crawled out through my eyes. It's barbed and rough with splinters and it's made out of steel wool.

I don't know why I feel bad about this place. Nothing good ever happened here. Nothing. And the money that's gone, it was probably less than a hundred bucks. Chump change. But I do feel bad, feel bad enough to cry.

I hear Tarasco come to the doorway. He stands there

looking at me. I look up at him and say, "It's gone, homie. Goddamn, even the getaway stash is gone. Another couple of days and all we would've found were ashes and sand. We just spent two hours crossing the sand for nothing. Big waste." He stands there, silent, a statue. "Man, come in here, and sit down, huh? We gotta think about what's next."

He comes in and sits across the small room, his back against the wall like me.

"Maybe there was another reason for coming," he says finally.

"Don't get Indian on me," I tell him. "The Big Spirit ain't coming to the rescue."

"You left your box at Teacher's," he says.

He's right. I forgot to even look for the box of things I'd taken from the house. Even with my face in shreds, with the cops and dealers bearing down, leaving that stuff makes me sadder than anything. I can't explain it. A goddamn feather, a couple of pictures, a comb she used, some religious statue that belonged to her mother, worthless shit, but it makes me feel like the last bit of everything has just been pulled out of my chest. I'd cry if I could.

"We could go back and get it," he says.

"No," I say. "I'm not going back there. And you'd be a sucker if you go. They'll be waiting for that."

"Maybe we had to come back here so that we'd find that there's no other place to go."

"Just let me think," I tell him. My head feels like it's bursting and the thing is that even though I know I should be running down what we should do, I just keep looking at the floor and the shadows and it's like looking into a blank screen in my head and the memories are playing on it, the early ones, where my mom is still young and I'm still a little kid, before the men, before the one who did things to me. She tried, so I never blamed her. Damn, she tried. She worked at it. But it's too goddamned hard.

"When we first came here," I tell Tarasco, "my moms took me to school. I'd never been, you know? I didn't want nothing to do with it. So the first day, the first chance I got, I split. I just went home. I sat out on the steps till she came home from working. She was worried because they'd called her and told her I'd gone missing. But she didn't give me a hard time about it. Instead, she told me that if I went back, she'd wait for me outside all day. And so we made the deal. I'd go back and she'd be there so that I could see her if I wanted. She stayed out there all day. It worked. I wasn't spooked after that." Tarasco doesn't say anything and we sit silently while the shadows work weird tricks between us.

Somewhere in there, I nod off and I dream that I'm moving in the dark. I can't see anything, like on one of those rides through a haunted house, only in this dream, there's no ghosts or goblins, no chainsaw killers, only sounds like moans and things being dragged, a metal door clanging shut, the sound of a key turning, and I keep feeling like I'm about to fall, that this thing I'm on, whatever it is, is about to run into something and I keep realizing in between being distracted by the sounds, that I'm not in control and then I jump awake, and Tarasco is still sitting across the room from me. He's awake. He's not watching me. He seems to be looking at the square of fading light on the floor, almost like he's watching a goddamn fire.

"How long I been asleep?"

"Not long," he says. "You keep waking up."

"We gotta go," I say using my legs to push myself up against the wall. It's not working too well.

"Something's happening," he says. "I've been listening to the sounds. Trucks and voices."

"Around here?"

"Out there," he says.

We get up and creep out the back instead of taking the chance of walking out the front door. It's eviction day, I guess. That's what Tarasco's been hearing, what I've been hearing in my sleep. There's a crew of deputies and ICE assholes out there making their way through Duros. They've hired some poor Mexicans too. They are going door to door to make sure everyone is out. When they find an occupied place, they march in and start pulling things out on the front yard, furniture, the odd mattress, clothes in black trash bags. It's old ladies and kids mostly. There's a lady who's hysterical, asking one of the wets what will she do with her kids. The wet just looks at her, embarrassment on his face, and he says "*lo siento*" and pulls his arm away from her like she's got leprosy.

One of the deputies comes up and says, "Miss, you're going to have to stand over here. You keep interfering with the workers and we're going to have to cuff you. You don't want that, lady." There's a snot-nosed kid clinging to the woman. He doesn't cry, he just watches with his eyes big and scared.

"*¿A dónde nos vamos?*" she asks the cop again.

"*No hablo,*" he says to her as he points where he wants her to go stand.

A cop notices us and he waves us over as he starts in our direction. I'd run if I could. Instead we just stay put and wait for him to get to us.

"What're you two doing here? Can't you read the signs? This place is closed. We've had a lot of trouble around here. We don't need any more." He's talking about the fires. The gloomy smoke hasn't stopped rising all day.

"We just came to get some things," I tell him.

"You've got a few minutes to do that," he says. "Don't get caught here after dark. We got arsonists on the loose and my deputies aren't going to spend a lot of time asking questions. You get me?"

Tarasco nods. The cop looks at me a little squinty-eyed. "I know you?"

"Don't think so," I say.

"What happened to your face?" While I'm trying to come up with a good lie, the lady with the kid starts wailing and the sheriff turns to see what the commotion is. "Jesus," he says, "don't you people know when to quit?" He takes off towards the old woman. "Just get on out of here," he says giving us the brush off.

"Let's go to my house," Tarasco says. "We can wait there until dark. Then we can move unseen." I don't argue with him. I'm tired, my legs got no spring, and I feel like I've got a fever. I need to sit down, catch my breath. I feel like I might pass out.

Tarasco's place is even more of a wasteland than my

trailer. It's covered with trash and there's a sloppy pile of whiskey bottles. His moms was a hardcore drunk. All you had to do was take a look at her. But she must have been world champ from the look of this toilet. It makes me sad for the kid.

"Where'd she go?" I ask him.

"I don't know," he says.

"Yeah, don't feel too bad, bro, don't feel too bad. I'm in the same boat as you. I'm an expert at having fucked up parents who leave."

"It's better that she's gone," he says.

"Why's that?" I ask him.

"Now she can die. She's wanted to for a long time but I held her back. That's why she was angry with me. Now she'll be able to find a hole and let it come."

"Damn," I say, and I mean it. "Maybe that's what most people want."

"No," he says. "My grandfather didn't want to. The people where I'm from don't want to."

"Yeah, well, I wouldn't know anything but the people in this shit hole. Beats the hell out of me why you'd stick around unless you wanted to die, slow or otherwise."

Then, out of nowhere, no warning, nothing, Tarasco bends down and picks up one of his whiskey mom's bottles and flings the fucker right through the back window. Everything crashes down, broken shards of window, thick brown chunks of bottle. And then the crazy *chaca* bends down and picks up more of the bottles and starts throwing them at other windows, against the walls, at the ceiling and floor. And it makes some kind of sense to me, to just break all this shit, and I bend down, weak as I am, and grab some bottles to throw. And the two of us shoot the bottles at everything, the broken glass showering down at our feet and in our hair. Feels good to break this shit, to break it all. I want to grow big as God and grab all these awful trailers and chunk them at the mountains and at the towns, I want to crush creation like goddamn Godzilla, just walk around stomping all this shit into dust, into the desert, the people, the roads, the buildings, the trains, just drive it right into the sand so that it disappears and there's no sign that anyone ever lived, loved, suffered, or died in this fucking place.

Exhaustion. The light is gone. There's no moon. Tarasco and me sit, backs against the wall, the pieces of glass litter the floor like a desert after an atom bomb has burned it all. I look at him, the big *indio, mi hermano* somehow, and I think, one of us is going to die. One of us isn't going to make it. I'd like to believe it won't be me, but I don't know. Somehow this shit just spun out, like a wild drunken drive where you're speeding down the road and then something jumps out at you, maybe just a shadow or a sudden flash of light, and you hit the brakes and you just spin and weave until you collide with *it*.

I want to ask Tarasco if there's something they do when they get ready to die. I know he's not one of the Crazy Horse Indians. He's more one of those Pueblo types, farmers and whatnot. But they got to know something more than we do. I want to know, is there some kind of secret knowledge in me somewhere? Something left over from when my pop's pop's pop was living on some mountain down south, something that might've been passed down? Something that they tried to make us forget up in this motherfucker? Something they knew was dangerous, so they told us all we were stupid and that we were dirty and smelled bad and didn't belong anyfuckingwhere? Maybe it'll be me that dies and not Tarasco. But dying doesn't mean I got to go out with a whimper.

"Why are you always so quiet?" I ask Tarasco. "You never say much. Don't you got any stories? Aren't you *indios* supposed to be good at that?" He looks at me in his weird, quiet way. Not exactly like he's staring through me, but more like he's staring into me.

"We aren't all quiet," he says. "I'm quiet. I'm quiet because I want to keep my stories. I don't want them stolen."

"That don't make sense, bro," I tell him. "Nobody wants to steal your sorry stories."

He looks at me a good long while and finally, he says, "They take everything."

"Whatever, man. Tell me one of your stories. I promise not to steal it."

Tarasco thinks for a second. "My grandfather told me stories he made up. When I need to think or say something, I remember things he said. This is one he told me a lot.

"The story of small, red Fox and his brother Coyote. In the first days, Man and Fox and Coyote lived together. They hunted together and sat by the fire at night. It was the voice of the gods on earth, speaking to man and animal brother through the flames and warmth. But it was not enough for

Man. And the gods, seeing this evil in Man, gave Man over to his greed and lust for more. And man turned against his brother animals. Fox and Coyote were chased away from the fire. And Man created a line between the forest and the village.

Coyote and Fox, driven away, watched the fires from a distance. Fox told Coyote, 'I will go deep into the wilderness and hide. Man has lost Love.' Coyote said, 'I will go up into the mountains and cry to the gods and brother Man. They will hear me and repent their wrongs.' Fox told Coyote, 'it will be the end of you. Man no longer hears your cries.' But Coyote could not be convinced to go into the wilderness with Fox. The next night, Fox, hiding in his den, heard Coyote's song. He saw his shadow high on the mountain ridge, the moon above the clouds, the fire of Man below in his village. The song of Coyote was beautiful, a sad cry filled with all the emptiness of lost friendship and lonely love.

It was not long before Coyote saw a trail of torches winding up the mountain. Coyote was filled with happiness thinking that Man was coming to fix their brotherhood. But it wasn't so. They surrounded poor Coyote even as he sang, piercing him with arrows and spears until he fell dead, his song silenced in the cold mountain air. They took his coat. They took his tongue. Fox mourned for his brother Coyote, but he mourned silently. He mourned the blood spilled, the hatred and fear that it made forever. He mourned the new creation of the gods and man—the Hunt, the coldness that drives away Love."

"Not bad," I tell Tarasco. "I get it. Keep your head down,

right? Keep a lid on it. But I gotta like the coyote. Not because he missed man or any of that sellout bullshit. See, he refused to hide. He thought, fuck it, if I'm going to go out, I might as well go out telling the gods and man to go straight to hell. That's why they killed him. To shut him up. Nah, Tarasco, they may have us on the run, but they won't shut us up. Not forever, and if they do, they'll have to take me out like they did the coyote. Of course," I say trying to think it through, "Fox lives to fight another day. I guess it's not so simple."

And then there's a knock, a hard knock, a cop's knock on the front door. Tarasco and I freeze up, looking up not moving, not breathing, till we hear the Teach saying, "Banger, Tarasco, are you in there?" I look at Tarasco to tell him to keep his mouth shut and stay still, but he's already on his feet walking towards the door. He opens it and the Teach is standing there with a flashlight pointed at the ground.

"We've got to get out of here," he says. "There's cops all over the place. Your father's been arrested," he says to me. "Get up, get moving. We don't want to get caught here tonight."

§ § §

We're driving the dirt roads of Los Duros, the last time I'll see this place, this place I never wanted to call home, but that was my home for so long. I'm leaving my dead mom, the junkers and skinny dogs, the rusted barrels and shoeless kids who played tag using them as home base, the old dude who sold corn on the cob with butter and chili powder, the little rose garden some *abuelita* took good care of, the drugs, the beatdowns, the pollution, the smell of sand and dust and shit and garbage so thick it penetrated the thin aluminum walls of the trailer. So thick it got in your hair, in your mouth and throat so you didn't even take notice of it anymore. I'm leaving behind the sickness, the drunkenness, the tears, the only goddamn place I'll ever have a chance to call home.

And you'd think I'd be happy because who isn't happy if they get to leave hell? Only, I'm thinking you carry hell with you. And sitting in the Teach's truck, despite me trying to feel like I'm glad this shit town is being burned to the ground, I get this feeling like my lungs can't hold air, like my throat is a tight fist that reaches into my chest, wants to crush my heart, and I feel tears running down the cuts in my face and it's all I can do to force it all back down.

They're trying to say that the same arsonist who set the school on fire is setting the fires in Los Duros. That means it's open season on Mexicans. They're linking the killing of the two Minute Men assholes to the community, too. It's spinning out of control. There's talk of bringing in the state reserves, wholesale deportations. Even the goddamn governor is getting into the act. Before the weekend is out, they'll be blaming us for the wildfires up north.

"Where's my father?" I ask.

"He's in jail. He's gone and confessed to the shootings last night. He gave them the gun we found in the van. He's even confessed to burning down the school. God knows what he'll be confessing to before the day is through."

We leave Los Duros, fires still smoldering, the headlights off as we cut through the desert to avoid the checkpoints that the cops have set up.

"Why'd he do that?" I say. "No one asked him to do that."

"He's trying to help you," Teach says.

"I don't need it. I can take care of my own problems."

"You can't take care of shit," Teach says.

I don't say anything as the Teach drives us back to his dark trailer. We go inside and the Teach gets down to business. "Look, if your father wants to take this on himself, I'm not going to do anything about it. It's not my place, but I have to know what happened. I want to know how it went down, who shot who, and why." He looks at me, staring me down.

"Don't look at me," I say finally. "Ask him." I look over at Tarasco. I half expect him to start telling about some fox or coyote shooting some donkeys or eagle.

"So," the Teach says looking over at the *indio*, "what happened?" But Tarasco isn't talking. He's somewhere else, la-la land. The pressure's gotten to him. He won't crack, though. This is a *vato* who knows how to keep his mouth shut.

The Teach says, "I don't know if the cops are going to buy your father's story. Maybe you'll get lucky and they won't care much. One Mexican is as good as another. But you never know who's going to get nosy. Your father thinks that whoever you went to deal with won't come looking now that there's so much heat from the cops. I hope he's right." He stops for a minute, looking me straight in the eye. "He took blame for the fire at the school. Why would he do that?

It doesn't make sense. What's he know, Banger?"

"He doesn't know anything," I say.

"Nah, man, he knows something. Fact is, he knows more than you want to give him credit for. Look, I know he let you down, that he wasn't around, but he's willing to pay a price for that. The least you owe him is the truth. You might not get the chance again, understand? Your father is going to go away for the rest of his life and you're probably going to have to run. You understand what that means? Running? From yourself, from your father, from your own life, from the truth? If your father is going to pay for the ride, you might as well take it. You might as well clean the slate. Do it here and now."

He's right. Why lie?

"Tarasco shot them, but I dragged him there. It wasn't supposed to happen. I don't even know where those suckers came from, what the fuck they were doing there in the middle of the night." I look over at Tarasco. He's sitting there, no expression on his face, his eyes fixed. I can't tell if he hears us.

"There's more," the Teach says.

"Fuck it. I set the fire," I say.

The Teach rubs his hand through his scraggly beard, cocks his head to the side sighing something sad, something he didn't want to hear.

"We didn't just go to the trailer to pick up the little stash of dough my moms saved up. I went there because me and Oscar hid the video cameras and computers there the night we set fire to the classroom. It was our revolutionary act. Fuck them, right? Isn't that what you was always saying?

Me and Oscar, we figured they fired you, right? So we'd set their school on fire, we'd say something to them in the only way those motherfuckers ever seem to understand."

"That's not what I set out to teach you," the Teach says.

"Nah, you tried to teach us that we could make those videos and show people how things are for us. But what happened, huh? Nothing, right? They clipped you, shut you up. They rained down their bullshit on us, shut down Los Duros, kicked out the old women and the kids. They took Tarasco for a ride and roughed him up. Brought up the big mouths to shout about illegals. So fuck them. They pound on us and they don't think we're going to pound back?"

"You didn't pound anyone, *vato*. That's not the way you win."

"C'mon, Teach. There ain't no winning," I say back to him, and that's when I notice I got tears in my eyes, tears I don't know where they're coming from.

"You're right about that," the Teach says softly. "But there's living with respect, there's the fight, and fighting it with your *gente*, with your brains, your skills."

"We took the cameras and computers," I tell him. "We were going to pawn them but we never got the chance. Don't matter anymore. Someone broke into the trailer and took them, took everything."

The Teach shakes his head. "Damn," he says. "How'd this happen?" he asks no one in particular.

"What do we do?" Tarasco asks, the first words I've heard from him in a while. He's looking at the Teach like he believes he can get us out of this somehow.

"Clean out your cuts, wash up, and put on clean clothes.

We've got nothing to do tonight but wait," he says. "Cops, the goddamn Minute Men, all sorts of media out there looking for Mexicans. We'll sleep and then go see your father in the morning."

I shake my head. It hurts to move it, the dried scabs break every time my face twitches making blood and water leak out. "Nah, man," I say. "I don't have anything to say to that *vato*."

"Yeah you do, Juan."

"Like what? What are you going to tell me that makes me want to go to talk to him?"

"You ever hear of St. Dismas?"

"No."

"When they hung Jesus on the cross, there were two thieves, and one of them told Jesus, 'Hey, if you're god, why don't you get us off these crosses?' The other thief, though, he said, 'You shouldn't talk to him like that. We deserve this, but he doesn't.' The thief, Dismas, understood that when someone offers to pay the price, you should know what it means. It's up to you, but I told your father I'd be there tomorrow. I told him I'd ask you to come."

"I'll go," Tarasco says.

Teach nods at him. The Teach goes in his room and leaves us alone. I don't feel like thinking so I turn on the TV. California is still on fire. It's funny, that. One of the things the law is going to come down on my old man's head for is setting the school on fire. The cops would put me in some hole if they knew I'd done it. But here God has gone and set a match to the whole damned state and who gets to put his ass in jail? No one. The big guy never pays. Never.

All the little ants scurry around when he pours gasoline on the ant pile and they come out in flames, little goddamned ants driven out. Maybe they've got a fire department. Yeah, fire ants. Get it? Only it's not funny. Ants get crushed, they get burned, they get thrown out. And what's their crime? Working, getting food, whatever ants do, I don't know. But it isn't anything they should get punished for.

The way I see it, we're the ants. And God doesn't listen to ants. The cops, and the whites, the judges, the bosses, they don't give a shit what an ant's got to say. So all this St. Dismas shit, all this Jesus on the cross stuff, man, it don't mean anything. The Teach ought to know that. My old man ought to know that. Maybe he figures he can sacrifice himself and spring me and Tarasco, but it's too late for Jesus.

The TV news goes back and forth between the fires and the murders, the fire chief talking about the flames moving so quick and catching everyone by surprise, and then the sheriff talking about the drugs flooding the country and how violence is catching everyone by surprise, and then a politician and the Minute Man leader talking about the illegals swarming over the border and catching everyone by surprise. It's like the plague, only I don't have to worry so much because I'm one of the germs.

Nah, the Teach is wrong. St. Dismas was wrong. Nothing good survives the flame. They won't let it and I don't want it anyway. They got their gangs, we got ours. I look at the talking head. You want fire, we'll give you your fire. There's lots left to burn.

§ § §

Sun comes up. I haven't shut my eyes. Tarasco's asleep. I hear the Teach get out of bed and head to the shower. He comes out after awhile and he says, "Did you get any sleep?" I shake my head. He comes over and says, "Let me take a look at those cuts. We've got to get you some stitches before it's too late. You're going to get some kind of infection. It's a real mess. Go put some of that peroxide on the wounds. Put some clean bandages on. We'll go by the clinic, get you fixed up."

But instead of letting me up, he stands there looking at me. He's not the Teach right now, just a big confused dude looking at me like I'm some kind of sad riddle. Finally he says, "Did you burn that schoolroom because you thought that's what I'd want you to do or did you do it for the score?"

"It don't really matter, does it?" I say.

He keeps looking at me. He wants an answer. He's not going to let me get up till I give him one. I sit there for a minute not because I'm trying to give him a hard time. I just haven't thought it through is all. So I tell him. "I don't know, Teach. I don't know. There's probably something really wrong with me because I don't think about it that much. And when I do, it's all muddled up."

"You could have broken in and just taken the equipment. You didn't need to set the place on fire."

"I know," I say. "Oscar didn't want to, but I did it. All I know was that it wasn't enough to just steal. Just taking some shit. It wasn't enough that night. I was mad."

"About what?"

"I don't even know. That's the truth. Maybe because

they fired you. Maybe because of my pops. Maybe because of my mom. Maybe because it was so fucking hot. I don't know. I was just mad. And when I set the fire and watched it catch and grow, felt the heat of it on my face, it was like I was looking inside myself." The Teach just looks at me.

"I know. I'm fucked up," I say.

He keeps looking at me and I don't know what he's thinking. It makes me nervous. Finally, he says, "I'm mad too. The world's a mess. I wonder how everyone doesn't see it." He doesn't say it like he usually says things, sure and proud. He sounds sad, like he's given up something. For a minute, I feel like I've given up something too.

Even though the nurse asks me, no one really cares what happened to my face. They put some stitches on my cut, pouring some kind of disinfectant on and telling me I have to take some pills to make sure I don't get sick. It hurts like hell because they have to bust up the scabs and the bleeding starts all over again. "You're going to have some serious scars," the nurse tells me. "I wish you'd have come sooner. We might have been able to take better care of the wounds." I don't tell her anything. What's she know about my scars? After she gets done, I go out to where Tarasco and the Teach are waiting.

"They get you fixed up?" the Teach says.

I nod.

"Good," he says. "You ready to go see your father?"

"What do I have to say to him? Thanks for taking the rap? This makes us even? We're homies now?"

Teach says, "I brought something you left behind."

"What?" I say already knowing before I see it.

"The box you brought from your trailer. I looked through it. I found the letter in there."

"Did you read it?" I say.

"No."

"Well, you should've. Nothing but bullshit from a jailbird to a stupid kid."

"Why did you keep it then? Why did you take it the other night? Must've meant something to you," he says. I want to tell him some good reason, but I don't have any.

"Did you ever try writing him back?"

"Nah," I say. But I did. My moms didn't read or write too well. I was too young to write. My mom asked a neighbor, this young *vato* who went to school. But I got shy telling him what I wanted to say. Anyway, it didn't get done and far as I know that's the only time the old man ever tried to reach me. Although we did move a lot, from place to place, house to trailer to house. So who knows? He sure didn't hire a goddamn detective though.

The jail is the same one I spent the night in after the fight. It isn't anything special. You might think it was a strip mall or something. There's only two floors. The bottom where the cops have their desks and where they book you, take your fingerprints, all that TV cop bullshit. Upstairs is where they have the cells. They kept me separate from the others because I'm not 18 yet.

The Teach parks his truck and me and Tarasco get out. I can tell Tarasco is nervous. He keeps looking at the metal screens they've got all along the top floor so the cons can't jump out. He's licking his lips, the heat and fear making his mouth dry like mine. I keep wondering what the hell we're doing here. What's all this supposed to get done anyway? I can imagine my old man wants to see me but I don't think he'd've forced the Teach into this whole deal. He doesn't seem like somebody who's willing to beg. At least that's something. I figure if the *vato* knows anything, he knows how to do his time quiet without complaining.

Thing is, when we walk through the door and I see the big white cop sitting at the desk, his bald head down, the tips of his black cop glasses visible beneath his forehead, I get panicky, like maybe this whole thing is a trap, that the Teach has gotten together with the *jura* to get me and Tarasco here with no trouble. I don't want to see my pops, I don't want to be here. I think about running, just a thought, like a bullet through the brain--take off, run, head for the mountains Tarasco talks about. But there's no time because the cop looks up at us. His face gets this bored look on it, like he's just spotted dog shit before he stepped in it.

"We're here to see Juan Acuña. This is his boy."

"Who're you?"

"I'm these boys' teacher. I'm looking after them for the time being."

"Upstairs," the cop says not even bothering to point his fat chin in the right direction. He goes back to doing his paperwork.

We take the elevator up and step out. There's a long hallway, beige, no windows, just a ton of bright buzzing lights leading to an information booth. There's some people sitting on these small orange plastic chairs waiting to be called in to see their beloved jailbird. There's a woman sitting behind glass and we give her my pop's name and she has us fill in our names on a form and tells us to sit. They'll call us. I look at the sheet of paper we were handed. It's got all the rules you have to observe. You can't hand anything to the prisoner, can't touch the prisoner, can't talk loudly, must observe the visiting room police officer's instructions. Everything is written in capital letters, big and black, like they're shouting it at you because you're stupid.

And while I'm looking at the paper, I feel Tarasco shake in his chair, like he got spooked and almost bolted out of the thing. I look over and the dude, whose skin is so brown, actually looks pale—like he's seen a demon. He's staring after a cop who's got some punk in handcuffs and is walking him down the hall to who knows where. I can't see either of their faces because they've passed us. All I see is their backs. Tarasco is still staring at them, his face scared. I tell him, "You all right?"

He says, "He's the one."

"The one what?"

"The one who took me into the desert."

"The one who beat you up?" I ask him. The Teach looks over.

"What's wrong?"

"The jaguar," Tarasco says. His eyes are still staring even though the cop and the prisoner have disappeared behind a door.

"Hey, you alright?" the Teach asks again.

"He goes on about animals," I say. "It's some *indio* thing."

The Teach ignores me. He reaches over and puts an arm on the Tarasco's shoulder. "Who took you in the desert?"

But he's clammed up. "Juan," the Teach says, "I'm going to take him outside for some air. You listen for your name. I'll be back in a few minutes." He and Tarasco get up, but before they head down the hall, the Teach looks back at me. "Hey, Juan. Think about what you want to say to him. It may be the last chance you get. You think about that."

He takes Tarasco by the arm and they walk down the hallway, the *indio* like he's sleepwalking in a nightmare, the Teach looking like he doesn't know whether to shit or sing the national anthem. With them gone, with the Teach gone, there's no one forcing me to stay. I could pick up, head out and no one would stop me. But I stay put.

I think about the letter sitting in the box in the Teach's truck and all of the sudden I decide that I am going to talk to my pops. I've got some shit to tell him. I've got some shit to show him. He thinks he's saving somebody? Wait till I show him what I've got. Today, the old man's my prisoner. He's going to understand what he's going to do time for. I go down to the Teach's truck. I find the two of them sitting on the tailgate. The Teach looks at me and says, "C'mon, Juan, I thought you were going to gut this through."

"I am," I say. I go around, open the door and just need a couple. I stick the yellowed letter in my pocket with the picture of my mother. And real careful, I put the peacock feather in my pant pocket. It sticks out with blue eyes staring at the bright desert sun. The Teach and Tarasco watch me turn back towards the jail. I'm practically running because I got something now. I don't know what I'm going to say, don't know if there's any words that can get at it, but these things, they'll do the talking.

I go back to the chair, waiting with the other people. People with sad eyes and twitchy kids. But not me. I got fire in my eyes, fire in my guts. And I'm mad, madder than I've ever been. The cop behind the Plexiglas says, "Juan Acuña, Juan Acuña," like she's saying it once for me, once for my father. There's two of us. I follow the long yellow arrow painted on the floor to the metal detector. Nothing beeps and the white cop barely notices I've passed through. I might as well be a ghost. I keep following the yellow line leading me into a small room with five tables, each with three chairs around them. My father is already sitting at the farthest one away from the door. There's a cop standing behind him. There's another cop at the doorway and he nods at me as I walk towards the old man. He's in an orange jump suit, the words Riverside County Jail stenciled in big black letters. His hair is slicked back like he combed it when he was in the *pinta*. He isn't smiling, but his eyes look at me soft and he bring his hands up to the table and lays them flat like he wants me to see there isn't anything in them. The guard sizes me up and takes a few steps back. I look at my pops hard, hard like I want to stab him with my eyes, shank his ass before either of the pigs watching can do anything about it. But all I got is the peacock feather.

He says, "Thanks for coming."

"Wasn't my idea," I say.

"I'm glad you're here anyway." He puts his left hand on top of the right, like he's trying to shield it.

"The Teach told me about what you did and he said I had to come."

"Yeah," he says taking a look at the cop at the door. "Look, they aren't going to give us but fifteen minutes. I wanted to tell you a couple of things."

"I got things to tell you too," I say. "You're not going to like them, but I'm going to tell you anyway."

"That's what I want," he says.

"I want you to take a look at her, I say and I pull the picture out of my back pocket." The cop behind my old man says, "You can't give him anything." I say, "I know. I just want to show him a picture." The cop lumbers over and he takes the picture out of my hand. He looks at the front and then turns it over. "Okay," he says handing it back to me. I put the picture on the table facing my father and I look at him while he looks down at the picture.

"You even remember her?" I ask him.

He picks up the picture and brings it close to his face. "I took this picture," he says. "I took it before. You and your mom. You couldn't have been more than two or three there." His eyes smile a little, a faraway thing, like his mind has floated back to that time, like he's remembering something I can't and that makes me mad.

"It's all I got left," I tell him. "You took her from me, not that drunk-assed *chaca* that killed her. You did it."

He looks back at me and he says, "The day I took that picture was a good day. There weren't a lot of them because of me. I know that."

I want to tell him again that he killed her, but part of me wants to hear him tell.

"We took a little trip to Vacaville, to see one of her cousins. I don't remember her name. Funny. But your mother had grown up with her on a ranch back in Mexico and they hadn't seen each other in a long time. We borrowed my friend's car and drove up there from L.A. We took Highway 1. You cried because the drive was long. To get you to stop, we pulled over near Big Sur and I held your hand and took you over by the cliffs. Your mom was scared. She kept telling me, 'Hold on to him tight.' I told her, 'Come over here and look at the ocean.' But she wouldn't. She didn't like heights."

"I didn't know that," I say.

"You don't remember that, huh? The ocean, the drive? The sky was blue. I kept on hoping we'd see one of them *pinche* whales or something. But all there was was the ocean, big and blue, goddamn, bluer than blue. And you stopped crying. I picked you up and the two of us looked out there till the wind blowing cold made us go back to the car."

"There's no ocean in that picture," I say.

"No. We took that picture in your mom's cousin's backyard."

"How come you're not in it?"

"I should've been," he says. "Some stupid reason, I didn't like being in pictures."

"Yeah," I say. But it don't come out right. It comes out sad and puny.

"What's with that feather?" he asks me.

"She kept a few of them in a vase to make the place seem nicer. It didn't work. It was a shit hole."

He says, "I saw a peacock the first day I went looking for you. You know the one I mean?"

"Yeah," I say. "He ain't there anymore. The whole place is gone."

"He was a beautiful bird," he says.

"Yeah, well," I say, "not everything's gotta be shit."

"It made me feel good, seeing that peacock. Made me think I was on the right track."

"That's dumb," I say. But I take the feather out and put it on the table. The goddamn cop comes up to the table and picks it up. He gives it a sniff, like he's some kind of coke dog. He puts it back on the table. My father runs a finger over the little blue-green hairs of the feather.

"In the joint, everything's ugly too. *Vatos* do what they can to fix up their cells. Pictures, drawings. I knew this one dude named Adolfo who used to make these nice sketches on *paños*. La Virgen de Guadalupe, ocean scenes, people, whatever. He'd give them to his homies sometimes. I asked him to do one for me once before he got out. He drew me." He reaches in his back pocket and pulls out a white handkerchief. It's folded carefully. He opens it, holding it up for me to see. There's a sketch of my old man, only he's not old. It's a picture of a young *vato*, arms and chest all swolled up. There's an open window over his left shoulder with a bird sitting on the edge like it's ready to fly off. Underneath the figure of my pops, is written:

All This Time, They Could Not Keep My Spirit Behind Bars

"Is that true?" I ask him.

He says, "No. I wish it was. But it ain't. Not by a long shot, *m'ijo*."

"Don't call me that," I say.

210

"Alright," he says. "But you are my son."

"Yeah, in name only. That's all we've got. That's all you gave me. I go by 'Banger' on the street. Don't like Juan."

"Names don't mean much anyway," he says. "Fact is that most of what they tell you means something in this world, is bullshit. Names, money, getting laid, living rich and fast. Goddamn country and flag. All of it, bullshit."

"What matters then?" I ask him.

"Surviving, not letting them take your freedom. Watching your kids grow. Protecting them from the devils out there."

That one catches me right between the eyes. I can't even start to say why. But it's like I'm dizzy, like he's managed to get in behind my face into something deeper.

I try to get it back. I say, "Fuck that. That's all bullshit." And when the words don't come, I remember I still have the letter in my back pocket and so I pull it out and drop it in front of him. "That's the only time I ever heard from you. Why don't you write that on your *pinche* handkerchief?"

"I don't have any excuses," he says. "I used them up a long time ago. All I've got is these last few minutes with you. You probably won't want to see me again. That's alright. I understand that. If I could fix it so that I didn't have to see myself again, I'd do it. There's nothing I can do about what I did to you and your mom. There's nothing I can do to undo what's been done to you. All I can do is try to fix it so you don't wind up in here. You've lost a lot, *m'ijo*. But you still got a whole lot they can take.

"I know I can't tell you nothing. All I can do is ask you to keep away. Keep away for good. Don't ever come through those doors again. That'll be my peacock feather." The old man looks at me and sad as his eyes are, he manages a little smile. "Please," he says, "take the *paño*. Maybe it'll make some sense to you one day."

The cop comes over. He says, "You can't hand the boy anything." My father looks up at him and says, "It's just something to remember me by."

"No," the cop says. "No exchanges." And my father's face looks like it's being pulled into pieces. And for some reason, I look over at the cop by the door and I say, "Maybe he can give it to him? Then he could give it to me."

And the cop at the door says, "C'mon Ron, let the guy give his kid the handkerchief." My pop's guard rolls his eyes at the other cop. "Yeah, whatever. You can hand it to him." He points at the other cop. "But it's your deal," he says to his partner. "I don't want to hear any noise about it later." The other cop comes over and takes the handkerchief from my father. He says, "You can get it from me when you leave."

My father says, "Thanks, man. That's real human of you."

"I got a kid too," the cop says taking the *paño* and walking back to the door.

The cop behind my father says, "Okay, you gotta wrap it up. You've already gone over the fifteen." My pop keeps his eyes on me and then he holds out his hand.

"No contact," the cop says. "I mean it. I'm not going to get my ass chewed out. You already got your break today."

My father puts his hand down, his eyes locked on mine, sad, but a funny smile in them anyway. "Remember what I told you," he says.

"Yeah," I say. It's all I can manage. The cop says, "Okay, stand up." My father stands, his eyes still on me. He keeps looking at me all the way out the door, the same sad smile in his eyes. When he's gone, I pick up the feather and the picture and the letter. I walk towards the cop at the door. He says, "You want the handkerchief? I can always give it back to him later. If you want to say Fuck You, that'd do the trick."

And without saying anything, I take it out of his hand.

"Good choice," he says. And I head out to the hall where I find the Teach and Tarasco waiting on those stupid plastic orange chairs.

We head down to the truck and outside an old *veterano*, the man who hired my father to drive the van, is out there with Henry, the young guy in a wheelchair that helped the Teach out a couple of times in class. They have the same face. The old guy is Henry's father. The old guy waves at the Teach, he says, "C'mere." He's wearing a cowboy hat, smoking a cigarette. He's got a loud voice with an old school accent. We walk towards them, meeting the two men in the middle of the hot parking lot.

"We were just going up there to see about getting Juan a court attorney."

"Yeah," the Teach says. "He's going to need one."

"Goddamn," the old guy says. "They're going to hang him out to dry. Jesus Christ crucified on a Joshua tree. They won't leave anything for the buzzards. I know these *cabrones*. I know the sheriff and the district attorney. I been watching them for years out here putting Mexicans away. They'll throw away the goddamn key."

The Teach is nodding, wiping the sweat off his face with the back of his hand, drying it on his jeans. "Yeah, it looks bad. What can you do? He confessed already."

"Why'd he do that?" Henry says from his wheelchair. "Even if he did it, you don't need to give those bastards any help. They got their nooses ready. No need to put it around your own neck."

The Teach says, "This boy here is his son, Juan Jr. This big one, we call Tarasco." The old guy holds out his hand. While he's introducing us, I can see Henry looking at me like he's figured it all out.

"Leo," he says shaking my hand fast and hard like he talks. "I know your daddy. I gave him a job. Best worker I've got. Quiet, goes home at night. Gets to work early. Does what he's supposed to do. Most of all, he's a good man. We're going to try to do right by him. It don't look good like your teacher says, but we're not going to let them railroad him, I don't care what he said. These bastards will try to beat it out of you. I know. I was with Cesar back in the day, back when the Teamsters and that *cabrón* Reagan tried to use goons to break our heads. They tried but they couldn't break our spirit."

"Yeah, well I just forced Tarasco here to tell me what the cops did to him out in the desert," the Teach says.

"I remember," Henry says. "I was with Juan that day we found you. You were in bad shape."

"They beat him up, put him in the trunk of a squad car. Let him get good and thirsty and then tossed him out to find his way home."

"Son of a bitch," Leo says. "They can kill someone doing that."

"That's the idea, pop," Henry says.

"¡Qué pinche desmadre! Well, we won't let them get away with it," Leo says. "No way. They can give us all the chingadazos they want. But goddamnit, we're not going to back down. I know your daddy. He's my friend," he says looking at me again. "I've known guys like him all my life. Solid as they come. I trust that vato with my van, with the keys to my business. He made deposits for me all the time. I know people. I know what they're capable of. Your daddy didn't do this. I don't know why he's saying he did it. Like Henry says, they probably beat a confession out of him. These cabrones, these pinche Minute Men coming out here with their guns and their pot bellies trying to play policeman and then they get themselves in a whole lot of shit and of course they're going to blame the first Mexican they get their hands on.

"It's the indios and their casinos. It's the construction companies. They didn't like the trouble and then they bring in the politicians and stir everybody up. They bring in the wood, pile it up and then wait for someone to throw a match."

"That's the way they work," Henry says. "We've been talking to some people. We're not going to go away. They think they can shut down Duros, arrest your father on a phony rap and call it a day. But we're going to march."

Leo says, "That's right. I talked to your daddy's girlfriend this morning. She's all broken up, a real mess. She doesn't believe he did it either. You know her?" he asks me.

I shake my head.

"Yeah, the two of you aren't too close, huh? Well, he's going to need you now. You got to put whatever there is between you away. Me and my boy had lots of trouble. It's never easy, but *familia es familia.* It's a damned shame, all of this. Your daddy was getting it together. A little house, a job, a girl. I know he was looking to give you a home, make things right." He takes off his cowboy hat, mopping his sweat with a bandana. He shakes his head. "A real shame."

Henry's been staring at me the whole time and he says, "What happened to your face?"

"He got in a fight a few days ago," the Teach says. "Got the worst of it."

"I'll say," Henry says staring at my wounds.

"Look," the Teach says, "these boys are tired. They've been up all night. I should take them back. They need some rest."

"Yeah, sure," Leo says. "That's a good idea. Get some rest. I'll call you later with the plans for the demonstration. You know something," he says putting his hat back on. "It'd be a good thing if Juan Jr. says something at the rally. That'd be real good. Let the people know that Juan's a family man. You too, Teacher. The kids and the parents will want to hear what you have to say. We're not going to lay down on this."

"Yeah," the Teach says. "Look, we're going to go." He shakes Leo's hand and then Henry's hand.

"Okay," Leo says. We leave them in the middle of the parking lot and walk to the Teach's truck. As I get in, I look back. Henry is still staring.

The Teach looks like he's not sure about another march, but the idea of getting one more shot to talk to the *mojados*, the sons and daughters of *mojados*, the white people, the power people, the ones who run the schools, the cities, the desert, the world, is more powerful than his doubts. He still believes in a peaceful revolution, a Zapata with a video camera instead of a gun. Even with all that's happened— my old man in jail, blood on our hands, his getting fired, Duros in flames, the people out on their asses—the Teach is still hoping. But nothing's changed. Nothing ever will. It's too late for Zapata, Teach. Too late for Cesar. Too late for my pops. Too late for Tarasco. Too late for me.

He says, "I'm not going to tell you what to do, Juan. I'm not going to tell either of you," he says looking at Tarasco and me. "But this rally's going to go down. Leo called. Tonight, a candlelight vigil that will start at the park and end in front of the jail. I'm going to say some things that people need to hear."

I can't take any more, and I say, "You gotta be kidding. The only ones responsible for my father being behind bars are me and Tarasco. And the old man for thinking he can change what happened to me and my moms by confessing to something he never did. I'm not going to listen to any of it. Nothing's ever going to change, get it? Five years from now, I'll be dead or in jail right next to the old man. And those *mojados* out there, they'll be in the fields. The men will still be getting drunk to forget that they have to eat shit every day. The women will still be sweating it out, getting beat on or treated bad because their men don't have no one else to take it out on. Kids will still be on the streets, still be dealing, still be using, still be fighting, still be fucking, still be waiting to get old, poor, or die young. And you know it, Teach. You know it. Don't tell me you don't know it.

"You know what you are?" I say to him. "You're like the *coyote* Tarasco's *abuelo* told about. Howling on the mountain, yelling at the gods because they set it up so someone's always on the bottom, someone's always on the outside, and it's our bad fucking luck that we're the ones that are doomed."

The Teach looks at me, his eyes on fire like the fires sweeping L.A. "That's your pain talking, Juan. That's your anger. And you got a right to feel it. You wouldn't be human if you didn't feel it. But you've got to put it to use in the right way. Not against your people. You use it for your people."

"And who're my people?" I ask. "You? Tarasco here? The *mojados* sleeping in the parking lots? Man, I don't belong to any of them and they sure as hell don't belong to me. I don't have any people. I don't have a country. The U.S., Mexico, that old school *Aztlán* trip the *veteranos* like to talk about when they're drunk on a Saturday night? Nah, *vato*. Only thing I can see that I belong to is the desert and myself. And now my old man's taking the rap for me so I guess I don't even have that. When it's all said and done, if you got an ounce of *sesos*, you'll say fuck the U.S. and fuck Mexico, fuck being an *indio*, a *chaca*, or an American or a wetback. Run off and make your own country in the desert mountains. Maybe you can protect that. Strike at anyone out there who even thinks about taking it. If that's what they want, there's lots left to burn. There isn't any forgiveness. So fuck it then, we'll live with that. Get it? Too late for Jesus, Teach, it's too late for Jesus."

He looks like I just went and popped him in the face. "You're wrong, Juan. You just can't see it yet. You've been through too much and they don't want you to see it. They've worked to keep you from seeing it, to keep you in the dark, you, me, your father, Tarasco, all of us. They've made it so all we do is wander in the dark. We need to teach ourselves, each other, how to see."

But he's wrong. Because I'm not wandering in the dark. I see it all clear. I see it clear as the fires burning up the houses in the California night. I can't go to that rally and lie. I steal, I burn, I fight, but I don't lie, not like that. The old man wants to do his time by doing my time and I can at least respect that much. My father looked me in the eye and told me the truth. The only other person who'd ever done that for me was the Teach. But this time the Teach is wrong.

No one does anything for anyone. My pops is doing what he's doing because he needs to do it for himself. The Teach is here in Califas with us *nacos* because he's got the need to change some minds, maybe some lives, because of whatever fucked up shit happened to him when he was a kid.

If I were to get up at that rally and talk about what a good man my father is, I'd be lying, lying about what I've always thought about him, about me blaming him for my mom and for what happened to me. I'd be a liar because I'd be pretending I'm innocent. It'd be an act. Pure bullshit put on to change someone's mind about us. And that isn't going to happen. The Teach can believe that fairy tale if he wants.

But I'm not. I'm good and goddamn guilty. I'll be guilty of a lot more before it's all over. If not killing someone or stealing, it'll be of drinking too much and being a prick to my kids, or being so angry I pass it on to my children or some other poor suckers. I got this thing burning in me and it ain't done burning.

What I learned from my father coming back and giving himself up for me, is to make sure I don't wind up paying for no one's sins but my own. I don't know if that makes sense, but it's got to, because it's all I can come up with.

I look over at Tarasco. He's still zoned out, like he's looking from somewhere up real high where he can see far into the distance. Or like he's looking into the past. He's been spooked since it all came down, and then seeing the cop that took him into the desert, seeing the prison, all that, was too much for him. I'm thinking his running days are over, over before they started. Not me, though. I tell him, "Hey *vato*, I don't know about you, but I'm not sticking around. I'm not going to get involved with this circus, this making speeches and marching and all that. I had some business with my father. That's done with. If you want to roll out with me, I'm good with that. You're about the only fool I can trust."

And while I'm saying this, I feel something click in my chest, in my goddamn throat, from the idea that this kid's the only friend I got. Like he's my brother or something. Only I can't tell him that so instead I go quiet. He doesn't say anything for a while. We just sit in the dark.

And then, "Where are you going?"

"I don't know."

"When are you going?"

"I need to rest tonight. But tomorrow, while the Teach is at the rally, I'll slip out."

"You shouldn't go anywhere until you know where you're going."

"Hell, man, I ain't never known where I was going. But at least I know I gotta go. That's something."

The next morning, I tell the Teach that I'm not going to the rally. He says that he understands, that he respects my decision. But he still wants me to show up. "You don't have to speak. But you should see for yourself that the community cares about your father, that they can come together peacefully and with dignity and demand justice. You know where justice begins?"

"No," I say.

"It begins with the basic principle that everyone's humanity must be recognized. Injustice only thrives in the persistent denial of the other's humanness. The denial of justice is a refusal to see the man behind the skin color, or clothes, or religion, or funny accent, or whatever."

"I'll think about going," I say.

"Good," the Teach says. He looks over at Tarasco who is still asleep. "How's he doing?" he asks me and I shrug. "He's usually quiet, but this is something different. He's the one that I think should probably stay away from the rally. He needs to work things through. He's strong, but he's also vulnerable in a way that you and me aren't."

"How do you figure?" I say.

"He's not cut out for this place. He should be back in the

mountains where he came from. There's no way for him here. It makes me sick, the way it works. His mom brings him here and when it's too much for her, she splits on him. It's fucking wrong."

Me and Tarasco ride up to the rally point. There's a couple of hundred Mexicans in the park. Some of them are holding Mexican flags. A few have hand-painted signs reading JUSTICIA PARA JUAN! and WE ARE HUMAN, and NO PEACE WITHOUT DIGNITY. There's a small platform with a microphone and a couple of speakers set up under a tree. Then I notice the counter protesters. A group of Minute Men holding an American flag and signs that say ILLEGAL IMMIGRATION = DRUGS, CRIME, TERROR, and WHAT PART OF "ILLEGAL" DON'T YOU UNDERSTAND? AMERICA FOR AMERICANS. There's a couple of news crews to record the party, gold-haired bimbos holding microphones, ready to tell the world that the aliens are marching. Standing by are about 8 or 9 cops, billy clubs at the ready to restore order, their order, Minute Man order. They are here to douse the other California fire, the one burning its way through this desert. They use gasoline. It's their only idea.

I watch the Teach shake hands with people. Lots of them are kids I know from school. There's parents, and some migrants, probably dudes my father picked up in the van. There are some college punks too. And on the platform is Leo and Henry, and the chick I guess my pops was with. It's funny, it kind of makes me feel good for my old man that people would show up for him. No one would have showed for me. And I know I should be the one behind bars. I know that.

The Teach goes up to the mic and leads the crowd in a *¡Qué Viva!* cheer. The crowd cheers Cesar Chavez, it cheers Mexico, it cheers the USA, it cheers *La Raza*, and finally it cheers Juan Acuña. The Teach yells about police tactics, calls for a fair hearing of my father's case, claims that he has been railroaded and that he is paying for the sins of all the *mestijaze* and undocumented labor in the state. "He is nothing but a symbol to these people," he says pointing at the Minute Men protestors, who are doing their own shouting. They scream, "Go Home, Mexicans!" and "Protect Our Borders!" and "America for Americans!" and basic stuff like "Shut Up!" and "Fuck You!"

The Teach keeps up the attack. "Juan Acuña is just an empty receptacle for these hate-mongers. They want to pour all their fear and anger and hatred into that empty can. But you know what? Juan Acuña is no empty can. He is a man with a heart, with a family, with a good and decent character. We won't let them empty him out and fill him with their vile meaning. They want to condemn him and in condemning him, condemn all of us. We won't let them," he yells to the crowd. "We can make a difference. We can deny them this violence that they are attempting to perpetrate on the body Chicano! C'mon, *gente*! *¡Sí se puede! ¡Sí se puede! ¡Sí se puede!*" And the crowd begins to chant along with him. "Let's march down the streets of Thermal. They will hear us because we refuse to be shouted down by the forces of bigotry."

He jumps off the stage and walks through the crowd.

They make a way for him and shake his hand as he passes. The group begins to form into a long line that will snake its way to the jailhouse. As the Teach and Leo and Henry and my pop's girl pass the Minute Men protesters, they begin to chant, "Murderer, Murderer, Murderer." One of them, a big white guy wearing a U.S. flag T-shirt, grabs at the small American flag that Henry is holding in his hand. He is wearing his Marine uniform, and when the guy makes to take the flag, Henry grabs his arm and the two begin to struggle. And then I watch as Henry falls out of his chair, and then a scuffle breaks out, and Mexicans are swinging at whites, and the cops join in the fight, slugging at brown heads, whatever brown head it happens to be. Women, children, it doesn't matter.

The reporters are busy filming and doing their own yelling into their mics. And it makes me realize that the Teach is only half-right in saying that the whites want to use my pops as an empty can that they can fill with their own meaning. The whole truth is that the Teach and Leo and the others want to do the same thing to him too. He's just an empty poster board that each of them can write their own slogan on. Nobody gives much of a shit what happens to him the man.

For the first time, I feel sorry for my father. I realize he hasn't just given up his freedom to take the blame for me, but he's given up something just as important--the hope of being able to decide who he is and what he stands for. I ain't going to let that happen to me.

"Let's go back," I tell Tarasco. "I've seen enough of this circus. I know how it ends." But Tarasco doesn't make a move, either to come with me or to go down and join the fighting. He's frozen. "You going to stick it out, *vato*? I can understand that. But you should come with me. Hell, we could go down south, find that mountain of yours." He looks at me, and I see in his eyes that he can't go anywhere. He'll wait here for the Teach. He'll wait as long at it takes because that's the way that crazy *indio* is.

"Listen," I tell him, "I'm going to leave something for you to do for me. It won't take a lot, but it's important. You'll find it on the Teach's table."

He nods his head. I hold out my hand and he takes it, drawing me in until he gets his arms around me. The big *chaca* squeezes me with all his might until I can hardly breathe. "You're my brother," he says. He let's me go but I still can't hardly breathe.

"Yeah," I say. "Yeah. We're brothers me and you. You take care of yourself. Take care of the Teach. He's crazy, but he cares and there's lots worse things than that."

I head off, leaving the marchers and protestors and cops to continue their endless fight. My father's house isn't far from the park. I walk there and pick up his truck. I have wheels now. I can move. I can get out of here. But before I leave this desert, I drive to the Teach's trailer. I've been thinking about the peacock feather and how my pops told me that seeing the peacock made him feel better because he figured that at least there was one beautiful thing where I lived. In the Teach's trailer, I take it out of the box of my other stuff. I put it into a big manila envelope the Teach has lying around. On the front of the envelope, I leave a note for Tarasco and the Teach. I write, "Please give this to my old man. I'm not sure what it means, but he will."

As I head out of Thermal and Mecca, I think that I don't have a past or even a future. What I got is now. The Now is empty, but maybe that's a good thing because I don't want someone else to fill it. I don't have a country, I don't have a people, or a family. I don't have love, or forgiveness, or memory. What little I had of that, I left in that envelope for the old man. Landless, lawless, but at least not hunted. Maybe I'll go down south and find Tarasco's mountain myself. When I do, I'll climb it like *Coyote* and howl at the gods.

87005750R00136

Made in the USA
Columbia, SC
16 January 2018